NICK EI

BLACK REEF

Seaward Publishing

BLACK REEF

By Nick Elliott
Published by Seaward Publishing
Amazon Edition
Copyright © Nick Elliott, 2018

ISBN 978-0-9929028-5-8

To the memory of my parents,
Walter and Kathleen

"I think when you've travelled around a lot in Africa, you understand something that many people here don't recognize: the extraordinary power that is Africa at village level - at community level."

Stephen Lewis, Canadian politician

"Going up that river was like travelling back to the earliest beginnings of the world, when vegetation rioted on the earth and the big trees were kings. An empty stream, a great silence, an impenetrable forest."

Joseph Conrad, Heart of Darkness

INTRODUCTION

It's the question every author is asked: what prompted you to write a book? Setting aside the fact I'd had it in the back of my mind for years, what prompted me to get started on *Sea of Gold*, the first in the Angus McKinnon series, was the idea of recording some of the more interesting, outlandish even, events of my career in the shipping business. I wrote out a list and realised that if I reshaped, embellished and dramatised all this material I might have the makings of a thriller. 'Write what you know' is the adage, and that's what I would do. On a trip to Morocco, I bought a red notebook at the airport and started writing detailed notes. At this point it just seemed like fun. After all, I told myself, I don't actually have to go through with it.

The next milestone was a trip to Greece specifically for research. By this time I was fully committed to the project – to finishing the book. And finally, two years later, *Sea of Gold* was published.

Although gold, as the title suggests, is an important element in the story, I'd never thought of gold as a thread which would run through the whole trilogy: *Sea of Gold, Dark Ocean* and *Black Reef*. But unintentionally, that's what happened. Gold, I realised, had become a metaphor for the greed and the lust for power that the villains in the stories had in common. A golden thread was being spun.

But what about the protagonist? Angus, an ex-seafaring Scot, born in Hong Kong and based in Greece, appeared in my imagination without much trouble. I've spent most of my life in and around ships and ports. I live in Scotland now but lived in Hong Kong and Greece for many years too.

What was not so straightforward was an early decision to write in the first person. I was warned of the difficulties of presenting everything from the main character's point of view only, but I wouldn't be dissuaded. Taking a leaf out of Len Deighton's books (his superbly drawn protagonists, Harry Palmer and Bernard Samson, are both presented in the first person), I was happy to accept the limitations of this style in favour of bringing the reader closer in to Angus's own character, his opinions, how he reacts to events as the stories unfold and his subjective view of the people and the world around him.

Angus might seem a reluctant spy. It certainly wasn't his chosen profession; rather, he stumbled into the murky world of espionage and frequently questions his own judgement in allowing it to happen. But as an outsider, he also feels able to challenge the precepts of the intelligence business. He's a tough, independent loner who has no qualms about going up against his superiors, not to mention his adversaries.

I decided to give Angus a private life, and a tragic back story. His domestic affairs, and particularly his relationships with women, are often complicated. He's no saint but he's a decent, reliable, morally sound guy. But like the rest of us, he's fallible too.

So, drawn into a world of intrigue and danger from the (relative) security of his marine claims investigation business, Angus finds he's unable to step back as events overtake him. And those events take him to all corners of the world: far from his base in Piraeus to the Black Sea, the Indian Ocean, Thailand and the Philippines, Hong Kong, Switzerland, Africa and of course, Scotland.

Writing of these places has been a big part of the enjoyment for me. 'Travelling – it leaves you speechless, then turns you into a storyteller,' said Ibn Battuta, the Muslim Berber scholar and compulsive explorer who travelled the medieval world in the fourteenth century. And I agree.

Nick Elliott, 2018

CHAPTER 1

Captain Luka Babic swung to and fro with the movement of the ship which, barely underway, was rolling heavily in the Atlantic swell.

'We should take him down, Padre. Will you help me?' I said. The body begins to smell when gases created by microorganisms are released and decomposition starts. Babic had been dead for a while. At this point I didn't know how long but the putrid smell, a bit like rotting garbage only much worse, filled the small dayroom we were gathered in. Three of those present held handkerchiefs over their nose and mouth. One of them, the ship's agent Lopes, had had to leave the room.

The last person to see the skipper of the *Dalmatia Star* alive had been the chief steward, who'd brought a meal in to him at around six the previous evening. It was still there on the captain's desk, untouched and distinctly unappetising.

'Sim, Senhor,' the padre replied. Father Manuel was an elderly man, seventy perhaps, who had been despatched from the Apostleship of the Sea, a charity offering pastoral care for the world's seafarers when their ships are in port, or as in this case, off port limits: the ship was hove to in international waters some fifteen miles off the Portuguese coast. The padre had travelled up from Setubal on the other side of the Rio Tagus, to join us, and seemed serene despite the difficult journey. It had taken us over two hours to reach the ship from port aboard a small harbour tug. In the rough sea conditions, boarding had been precarious, particularly for Father Manuel. The crew had lowered the ship's diagonal accommodation ladder for us but the tug's gunwales had slammed up against the bottom of the ladder with every roll so we'd had to use the pilot ladder which they'd lowered down to the boarding mark, a white and yellow rectangle painted onto the ship's hull. Then, helped by a man rope, we'd crossed safely to the accommodation ladder and on up to the deck.

The captain had been strung up using a leather belt. He must have placed it around his neck first, threading one end through the buckle to form a noose before tying the end of it around one of the arms of the sprinkler head which extended from the ceiling of his cabin and which itself was screwed into the pipes of the ship's fire control system above. Looking around I could see it was the only securing point high enough and strong enough from which to hang a man.

I had already photographed him from different angles including his face, oddly relaxed-looking now. I'd imagined bulging eyes and a protruding tongue but Babic looked at peace, something with which I might console his widow I thought.

The padre stepped up onto the stool reaching out to place a shaky hand on my shoulder as he did so. I guessed Babic himself would have stood on this stool before kicking it from under him in the last moments of his life. I put my arms round his waist and lifted him so the padre could reach up to remove the noose from around his neck. Close up the smell was overpowering and I struggled not to gag. Then between us we carried him from the dayroom into his bedroom and laid him on the bed.

Now there were just the two of us I examined the body and particularly the neck, more closely, taking photos as I did. He was wearing a white shirt with a captain's four straight gold bars on the epaulettes. One of these was twisted and two of his shirt buttons were missing. I checked the pockets of his trousers but found nothing. He was still wearing his shoes and socks. What does a man do before taking his life? Write a suicide note? I'd already searched his desk. Now I looked through the bedside drawers and the wardrobe and found nothing.

'What do you think, Padre? What should we be looking for?'

'Will there not be a post mortem examination?'

'Yes, there will. I just wondered if you had any observations to make.'

'Who am I to judge? That is God's work. Why, you think he did not kill himself? That he was murdered?'

'I don't know,' I said. I wasn't a pathologist but I'd seen a few things to make me wonder. 'Let's leave him in peace now.'

The padre said a prayer and marked Babic's forehead with the sign of the cross. We pulled a sheet over him and left, closing the door after us before returning to the dayroom.

Both the door into the passageway and the portholes were open, allowing the salty Atlantic breeze to blow through and clear the air. The three other men there were the chief officer, the ship's agent and a senior superintendent from the shipowner's office in Rijeka. His name was Vladimir Horvat.

'Can we get on with this?' said Horvat in his heavily accented English as we sat down. 'I have to get back to my office.'

'I have a few questions,' I said. I wasn't sure whether he had a reason for being obstructive or whether this was just his normal manner. He was a heavily built, muscular man with a large head, cropped blond hair and small dark eyes below barely discernible eyebrows. His most noticeable feature was his mouth. His thin lips framed a slit like a tiny letterbox. His teeth, when they showed, were stained yellow. He'd been chain-smoking since I'd first met him earlier in the day and he was lighting up another cigarette as we spoke.

We'd come out to the ship together, having met in the Lisbon agent's office that afternoon. I'd flown direct from Edinburgh and he from Rijeka via Frankfurt. Since we'd met his behaviour had been abrupt to the point of open hostility.

'Did you know Captain Babic well?' I asked.

'What has that got to do with anything?'

'How long had he been with the company? Was he a reliable officer? Was there anything in his medical records or his reports to suggest he might be depressed? Suicidal? I'm trying to build up a background picture of what might have led up to this.'

'Not that I know of. Why don't you ask the chief mate here, or the other officers?'

'Because I'm asking you,' I replied, my patience wearing thin. 'I'll get to the crew later. Right now I expect you to answer my questions.'

'Babic was an average master,' he said grudgingly. 'We had no bad reports from him or about him. I looked at his medical report before I left the office. He was fit for duty.'

'What do you know of his personal life, his domestic situation?'

'He was married to a Greek woman. More than that I do not know.'

'Children?'

'Yes. Two boys, I believe.'

'And they live in Thessaloniki, is that right?'

'Yes.'

'Why do you think he hanged himself instead of just jumping overboard?' I asked, as much to myself as to the others.

The padre replied. He'd been thinking about it. 'Who knows, Senhor? Maybe drowning alone in the ocean with no one to find his body was a prospect he could not face.'

I wasn't getting far with my questioning. Babic had a reason for ending it all, whether it concerned his personal life and state of mind or something else. That's if he had been the one to end it. I persevered with Horvat.

'I want to know about this voyage,' I said. 'She loaded in Trabzon. Is that right?'

'Yes.'

'Second-hand vehicles, machinery and spare parts for discharge where? I know she was ordered to wait here off Lisbon for further orders but what's her final destination?'

'I don't know.'

'Look, Horvat,' I said. 'We can do this the easy or the not so easy way. I have authority from the ship's insurers and by proxy from the flag state, to conduct an initial investigation on their behalf. I'm not leaving the ship until I have some answers, and neither are you.'

'You cannot order me around.'

'Stop me,' I challenged him. I'd told the agent this might take some time but I was still hoping to get ashore before midnight. There was a big storm the other side of the Atlantic spinning its way eastwards. The weather was worsening, which was why we'd taken a tug and not the agent's launch. There might come a point when it was too rough to get back to port.

I tried a different tack. 'Just answer my questions. They shouldn't present any difficulties if you have nothing to hide. Alternatively, we can tell the chief officer here to bring the ship into port. He has a Master's licence and the agent can order up a pilot.'

'That will cost money. We will incur port and pilotage dues unnecessarily.'

'Such costs will be recoverable under your P&I cover,' I reminded him. In the shipping industry protection and indemnity insurance is arranged through mutual associations known simply as P&I Clubs, in this case the Caledonian Marine Mutual Protection & Indemnity Association of Leith in Scotland, a Club formed in the late nineteenth century in the heyday of the British merchant marine. As a freelance marine claims investigator based in Piraeus, close to the biggest community of shipowners on the planet, most of my work came from Greek owners whose ships were entered with the CMM. The kinds of claims we handled were many and various. Cargo damage and collision liability, crew death and injury, as well as contractual fraud were just a few I'd been brought in on over the years. But I'd been called into this case because Croatia, for reasons of proximity, fell under my jurisdiction, and because of the last case I'd handled, which peripherally had involved the same shipowner.

'We are not taking the ship into port, do you understand? I will answer your questions but the ship will remain in international waters.'

'Good,' I said. 'You say you don't know her destination, yet the ship is carrying a full cargo of motor vehicles and machinery. I don't understand.'

'The cargo was purchased speculatively. A sale has not yet been finalised. Such situations are not uncommon as you will know, McKinnon.'

He was right but I wasn't convinced. 'Why did the ship head north after passing Gibraltar? Do the shippers expect to sell the cargo in north Europe? That seems unlikely.'

'This I do not know.'

I turned to the chief mate. 'I'd like to see the cargo manifest.'

He looked nervously at Horvat, who nodded his consent. The mate walked over to Babic's desk and handed me a plastic folder of documents. There was one bill of lading covering the whole cargo, a cargo manifest and a set of tally sheets from Trabzon, the loadport. The shipper was named as the Trabzon Logistics Company. In the consignee column on both the bill of lading and the manifest were the words, To Order, in other words, to be advised once the cargo had been sold. The cargo description stated second-hand vehicles.

I handed back the folder. 'I'd like a copy of the crew list too.'

Again, the nervous glance at Horvat, who again nodded his consent. I scanned it briefly. Twenty-four crew, or twenty-three now, mostly Croatian and Polish officers with Filipino ratings. 'I'd like a quick look around the ship now, then we can wrap this up,' I said.

'Is that really necessary?' Horvat demanded.

'Yes, it is.' I wanted to get a feel for the atmosphere, the condition of the ship. And I wanted to talk to the chief mate without Horvat breathing down his neck. Inevitably in my line of business, you met resistance if shipowners, charterers or whoever else might be involved in a claim or dispute wished to conceal relevant facts. I'd learned to recognise such behaviour and in this case it was blatantly obvious.

'You don't want to go into the holds, I hope. In this weather there's a risk of seawater damage to the vehicles.'

I couldn't argue with him on that. Seawater was already washing over the deck as the ship plunged into the swell. Opening the hatches would risk flooding the holds.

I addressed the agent, a middle-aged Portuguese man

who had been listening to our exchanges with interest. 'Mr Lopes, can you work with the tug and ship's crew to transfer Captain Babic's body onto the tug. It will need to be taken to the mortuary for the post mortem and until it's decided where he will be buried.'

'Can't we bury him here, at sea?' Horvat asked. 'It is the tradition.'

'No. A post mortem examination will be necessary. If his widow were to raise a successful claim against the owners, it would be for the CMM as the insurers to settle it. We need to establish cause of death. There may well be an inquiry by the flag state too. As I told you, I'm here to represent them as well.'

'Alright,' said Lopes. 'Let me organise it.'

The chief mate called up the bosun and two ratings to help with the transfer. Then he addressed me: 'Shall I take you around now?'

'I will accompany you,' said Horvat.

'No, I'll speak with the chief officer alone,' I said. 'You stay here and assist with the transfer of the body.' He didn't like being steamrollered, although I was beginning to enjoy it.

The chief mate, Mornaric, was also a Croat. 'What's your first name?' I asked as we walked out onto the main deck. I had to raise my voice now against the gale.

'Juraj, like George. Mornaric means son of a sailor.'

'Was your father a sailor?'

He laughed. 'No, he was a civil servant in the roads department.'

'How long have you been at sea?'

'Eighteen years now. I got my Master's ticket five years ago.'

'Have you had a command yet?'

'No. But I am ready.' He was in his mid-thirties, slightly built with dark hair and intelligent eyes.

'That's just as well,' I said. 'You'll need to be ready now. Let's go aft where there's some shelter.'

'Sure.'

We walked back towards the afterdeck. The *Dalmatia Star* was over twenty-five years old and showing her age now. The deck was pitted with rust and I wondered about the state of the shell plating, and when she'd had her last special survey. But that wasn't why I was there.

Ships make distinctive noises in heavy weather, especially when they're not underway. The *Dalmatia Star* groaned, clanked and screeched like some arthritic iron monster. We braced ourselves with our backs to the accommodation bulkhead. Across the heaving grey swell I could make out the coast, barely visible through the rain and murk. 'How long had you known Captain Babic?'

'Only this voyage. He joined in Thessaloniki.'

'I didn't know you'd made a call there.'

'We took on bunkers. And Captain Babic joined. He

lives there anyway. Lived there I mean.'

'Who did he relieve?'

'Captain Novak. You ask many questions!'

'It's my job. Was that a routine changeover?'

'No. Novak had only been on board a few weeks. I don't know why the owners decided to replace him.'

'Are you happy on board? You and your shipmates? Or were you, before the skipper's death? Was this a happy ship?' You can usually tell.

'I've been with the company since I was a cadet. Yes, it was a happy ship. But the company has many troubles, you know. And now the captain …'

'Tell me,' I said. I knew something of those problems but I wanted to hear about them from him. We'd headed back into the ship's accommodation to get out of the weather. He took me to the officers' mess and poured coffee for us both from a machine secured to the bar-top. We sat down and he glanced nervously at his watch.

'Relax,' I said, 'we have time.'

'You know we all have shares in the company,' he said. 'We are like a cooperative. It's unusual in the shipping industry I know, but it works well for us. At least it did until we had the problems.' He pulled out a packet of cigarettes and offered me one, which I declined.

'Do you mind if I do?'

'No, go ahead.'

He drew deeply on it and blew the smoke upwards. 'The company became a target for a hostile takeover. That is the right expression I think. I don't know the details but it all fell through. I think those behind it got into serious problems. But it left us with serious problems too. We had to sell half our fleet, that's six ships. They were fine new vessels, not like this old lady. But it seems that wasn't enough to get us out of trouble.'

He stood up and went over to close the door of the mess room. 'I don't like what we are doing now. This cargo, what is it for?'

'What do you mean?' I asked.

'Second-hand vehicles from Trabzon? Do you know about Trabzon?'

'I know where it is, but tell me.' Trabzon was a port on the Turkish coast of the Black Sea.

'It is from where NATO's ISAF equipment from Afghanistan and Iraq is returned to their countries of origin. It is flown in on big transport planes from the war zones then shipped out through the port. That is what we have loaded: American, British, German armoured vehicles.'

'What kind of armoured vehicles?'

'Armoured Personnel Carriers, also Bradleys I think they are called, and British Warriors. They look like tanks. Two landing craft, and crates containing rocket launchers and mortars, shells and missiles. I was down below this morning to check the lashings. In this weather I don't want anything heavy breaking loose. I tell you, you could start a war with our cargo.'

At that moment the door burst open and Horvat entered, bearing down on us, his face red. Mornaric leapt to his feet and backed away, his back to the bulkhead.

'What are you doing? This is my ship,' he shouted prodding himself in the chest for emphasis. 'What were you talking about here? Tell me!'

'I thought it belonged to the bank nowadays,' I said. 'Anyway, we're finished here.' Horvat was a volatile thug and I didn't want this to escalate. 'Has the captain's body been moved to the tug?'

'What? Yes, they have taken the body. I want to know what you were talking about.'

I got up and stood in front of him. He tried to push past me to get at Mornaric but I wouldn't let him. He was breathing his foul breath heavily into my face. I pushed him away and he stumbled backwards, fetching up against the bar.

'Calm down, Horvat. We were discussing the poor condition of this ship, and the troubles the company has. The mate is worried for his future. Now let's get ashore. I'm content for you to hand over command to Mornaric here. I've conducted a preliminary interview with him and he's shown me his Master's ticket and service record. So let's go shall we?'

His face was flushed with anger. 'I must report to my head office to see that they approve his promotion.'

'Good.' I walked to where the mate was standing and shook his hand. 'Congratulations, Captain Mornaric. I shall also report back to the insurers and your flag state that we endorse your promotion.' And before Horvat could argue I headed for the door.

CHAPTER 2

It was past midnight by the time the tug was moored back alongside the berth in Lisbon. Lopes, the agent, had arranged for the captain's body to be taken to the mortuary and said he would notify the port police. Horvat had resisted these arrangements but the collective force of the agent, the padre, the tug captain and myself had overcome his opposition. Finally though, he'd chosen to remain on board the ship.

The following morning I spent writing up my report, which I emailed to Claire Scott at the CMM in Leith. Claire was the CMM's Chief Operating Officer. She had asked me to report back to her direct on this case since she was handling the other end of it: namely the fallout from the attempted hostile takeover of Dalmatia Shipping that Mornaric had mentioned. It was a complicated legacy case that both Claire and I had been involved in some months before. Dalmatia Shipping was one of many shipowners to have fallen victim to a conspiracy by a cabal of Japanese and Swiss-based neo-imperialist gangsters making a serious attempt to wrest control of global trade. It had failed due to the intervention of the International Maritime Task Force, a low-profile intelligence agency attached to what was once British Naval Intelligence and was now merged into the Ministry of Defence's Intelligence Department. It had been set up as a taskforce to investigate the flood of maritime fraud incidents which reached epidemic proportions back in the 1970s. Its success in investigating these crimes secured its future and before long they were supplying intelligence to NATO and other agencies relating to piracy attacks off the east and west coasts of Africa and the South China Sea. It suited the IMTF's masters in the Ministry of Defence to retain its taskforce status. It allowed for greater flexibility, and less accountability too.

Claire had been enrolled into the IMTF straight from Oxford. She was a talented lawyer, and the CMM provided a perfect cover for her covert work as an intelligence officer. I had been enrolled into this shady organisation almost by default and, as I was now realising, separating my CMM work from my role as an IMTF field agent was becoming virtually impossible. The understanding had been that I would be hired to perform the "odd job" for them alongside my own business as a claims investigator, but it hadn't worked out that way. Instead, my life had become a series of often life-threatening events over which I seemed to have little control. The money was good though.

The CMM, as both the *Dalmatia Star*'s insurers and its legal counsel, was involved with the banks in restructuring Dalmatia Shipping and re-establishing it as a viable business. As part of the recovery plan some of their newer ships had been sold off but the task was far from complete. The whole process was further complicated by Dalmatia Shipping's unusual corporate structure, with directors and both shore and seagoing staff all retaining shares, sometimes also held by family members and sometimes inherited down through several generations. There was a ton of legal issues to be resolved and it needed a nimble-minded lawyer like Claire Scott to untangle the mess.

Now, after what Mornaric had told me, it seemed that the owners were covertly and illegally booking highly profitable but suspect cargoes at inflated freight rates in an effort to trade their way out of their financial difficulties. What they might not have realised was that such fraudulent practices would almost certainly void their insurance cover. Because only Claire and I were privy to the finer details of the case from all its many perspectives, I expressed these concerns to her in my report.

Then there was the matter of Babic's death. What had driven him to suicide? If it was suicide. Or had he been murdered because he'd threatened to blow the whistle on his employers' and fellow shareholders' nefarious activities? If so, I didn't hold out much hope for Mornaric's future prospects.

And what of Horvat's role? I expressed these concerns too in my report and sent it off by encrypted email.

In Lisbon the sun was shining and the streets were alive with tourists, shoppers, garishly painted tuk-tuks and dilapidated trams. I stopped to watch a group of black-caped students singing and playing their guitars. It was an easy city to love and the troubles of the *Dalmatia Star* seemed a lot further away than just a few miles off the coast. I walked on, getting lost, and finally sat down at a side-street café. As I was ordering a beer, Pedro Fernandes called.

'Hey, what's my old friend doing in Lisbon and not bothering to call me?'

'How are you Pedro? I was going to, believe me.'

'Ah, so he says. Listen, we need to talk – soon. Can we meet tonight?'

'Sure, that'd be good. Give me a time and place.'

'I'll get a table booked. Just tell the taxi where you're going. He'll know it.' And he gave me the restaurant's name.

I prized old friends like Pedro. Some I'd sailed with, others I'd met while working on cases over the years. They were scattered to the four winds but most had been seafarers at one time or another. The shipping business being what it was, some of these characters were above the law and others treated it as an inconvenience to be bypassed when the need arose. Pedro fell between the two.

***

I could see we were heading into the Alfama district, not so far from the port: a maze of narrow cobbled streets and ancient houses leading up a steep hill leading from the Rio Tejo estuary towards the castle. Originally it was outside of the city walls – a squalid ghetto where only the poor lived. As Lisbon's port grew, Alfama became the tough and deprived quarter, home to sailors and dockers, whores and pimps. It's thrown off most of its dodgy reputation now and become a trendy artisan district, but for me it had still managed to keep much of its dilapidated charm.

A mist had rolled in from the river as it often did at night in this city. The taxi stopped and the driver pointed up a poorly lit lane. I paid him off and headed up the cobbled pathway. At the top I could see lanterns and a gateway framed by thick foliage. As I drew closer I heard music and when I entered the place I saw a woman standing on a small stage. She was singing a melancholy lament to the accompaniment of two men playing teardrop-shaped twelve-string guitars. I knew I was hearing Fado: the blues of Portugal.

Pedro stood up from a table in the corner and walked, or more accurately rolled over to greet me.

'Come, my friend. Welcome. We'll eat, drink and listen to the music; then we can talk.'

He called for wine and a bottle of Dao red arrived,

which we consumed while waiting for the food. Then he ordered another bottle with the arrival, in a clay pot, of the *caldo verde* soup made from onions, potatoes and kale with a slice of smoked sausage sitting on top, the whole broth thick with garlic and olive oil.

'Good food for a cold night,' Pedro assured me as he ladled the stew into my bowl.

The singer had returned to the stage amidst enthusiastic applause from the diners. She was young, no more than thirty, beautiful and dressed in a low-cut black gown. The two guitarists sat either side but back from her.

'She is famous, this one. She has been singing Fado since she was eight years old,' Pedro explained. 'This is not unusual. It is in their heart and soul; not just theirs but all us Portuguese.'

She began singing and silence fell across the room. Her voice had a haunting beauty that commanded attention.

'She is singing of longing and grief, hope and despair. Our word *saudade* means longing. It symbolises a feeling of loss, permanent loss.'

Pedro was a sentimentalist, but listening, it was hard not to be moved. The meaning and emotion of the songs came through without me understanding a word of the lyrics.

A dish he called *Arroz de Pato* arrived next: duck with rice, cooked in red wine and crowned with more smoked sausage. 'The rice absorbs the juices of the duck,' Pedro informed me. He was a self-confessed gourmet with the figure to prove it.

The Fado singer took a break and finally the conversation turned to business.

'People are asking what you were doing on that ship yesterday, my friend.'

'Really, who?'

'I will tell you only what I have heard. Now I know it's a P&I case, for your CMM people, all above board, but these people seem to think you have another agenda. Like your Piraeus, Lisbon is also a leaky sewer, Angus. It always has been. So I hear things. It seems your friend Lopes, the ship's agent, was looking to supplement his income. He has told people that your questioning of the owner's superintendent was somewhat intrusive. You probed him about the cargo, where the ship had loaded and where she was going to discharge.'

'Come on, Pedro. It was routine stuff.' Pedro was a marine surveyor who'd been at sea himself for years. He knew the importance of putting things in context, of building a background picture when it came to a ship's condition, of the cargoes she carried, her owners' operational standards, their preventive, or more often, breakdown maintenance programmes, crew training and qualifications, and a host of other factors.

'Maybe it was,' he said. 'As routine as suicide can be, that is. And you and I both know that suicide rates among seafarers have more than tripled in the last three years alone.'

'Yes, and it's triple that of shoreside workers too, but that doesn't stop me asking what drove Captain Babic to end his life – if he is the one who chose to, that is.'

'What, you think he was murdered?'

'I don't know, Pedro. It's possible. Maybe the post mortem will tell us more.'

'Well, who can say?' Pedro wiped his mouth fastidiously with a white linen napkin to remove any trace of food or red wine.

'But to continue with these events I have learned of, there is a bank here, Banco Imperio. It is they whom Lopes reported to, through an intermediary I suspect, and it is they who have been asking questions about you. They are wondering if you are more than just a marine insurance investigator. Of course, I'm not going to ask you about that but let me tell you something about this bank.' He took another sip of his wine, turned round to see that no one was eavesdropping on our conversation and leaned towards me conspiratorially. 'The bank was established many years ago when Portugal still had an empire. They did much business in our African colonies, and in Macau too. Then during the war they were one of several banks here who were receiving gold from the Nazis in payment for wolfram, or tungsten as you call it, for the German war effort. You know what a kinetic energy penetrator is?'

'No, but you're going to tell me aren't you.'

'It's a type of ammunition designed to penetrate vehicle armour. Like a bullet, it does not contain explosives but uses kinetic energy to pierce the target. That is what the tungsten was needed for – to harden the steel. We exported great quantities of this mineral as ore to Germany and much of it was paid for in gold, gold that had been looted by the Nazis.

'You know that Portugal was neutral and one of the few centres of tungsten production. We sold the ore to both sides, the British and the Germans, and the German armaments industry was almost entirely dependent on supplies from Portugal. You're beginning to see the picture now.

'So because of this trade, Portugal became the second largest receiver of Nazi gold after Switzerland. At first payments were in currency, but then our central bank, Banco de Portugal, found that much of this was counterfeit and our president, Antonio Salazar, insisted that all future payments be made in gold. The Nazis helped themselves to gold from the central banks of the countries they invaded, and from individuals too – mostly from Jews.

'Now then, Banco Imperio, the bank that is showing such an interest in you, has been investigated many times over its wartime gold receipts, and has been heavily criticised, yet still it survives.'

'That's fascinating, Pedro, but why are they interested in the *Dalmatia Star*?'

'We can only speculate. They have received this information about your visit to the ship because they have some interest in her, and especially her cargo. Lopes believes the ship is carrying armoured vehicles and weapons too perhaps. What does this tell you?'

I wasn't surprised that Lopes had known. It hadn't been difficult for me to discover what the ship was carrying and any ship's agent worth his salt would have found out too, even though the ship was in international waters and not scheduled to discharge her cargo in Lisbon.

'That they're probably involved in the sale and purchase of illegal arms,' I said. 'And they don't want anyone poking around in their business.'

'Yes. At present that is all we can guess. And for what purpose you will ask. But I tell you this my friend, Banco Imperio and those who act on its behalf are not the kind of people you would want to sit down and have dinner with, never mind deposit your hard-earned money in. They are rich and powerful and they have a reputation for ruthless business dealings.

'Who owns the bank?'

'There is a veil drawn across their activities and the identity of their shareholders, even today. But there are rumoured to be Swiss banking interests involved, no doubt carefully hidden through proxies and heaven knows what. Just be careful in your investigations. Better stay away from them if I were you. Remember, this city also has a reputation. In the war German spies mingled in the same circles as British and American agents. Kidnappings and killings were commonplace. Some of that culture lingers still.'

'I shall be warned, Pedro.'

CHAPTER 3

Leith Links had been white with an early frost that morning as I'd walked over. I'd met Grant as he was getting out of his Bentley, one of many such cars of that marque he owned, outside the entrance to the office. Cameron Leslie, the janitor, had just emerged from the building to park it for him. Grant had invited me up to his office on the top floor of the old building and instructed his PA, Phyllis, to bring us coffee. He'd had his office redecorated since I'd last been here: still all muted tones of grey with black furniture but now some Impressionist prints on the wall, and the smell of fresh paint. Few, if any, would guess that the whole building housed a covert intelligence agency funded by and under the wing of the Ministry of Defence.

'So what's your take on this, buddy?'

'As far as the *Dalmatia Star* is concerned we wait, Grant, until we know where she's going. But Claire needs to be in on this discussion. After I sent her my report I picked up something regarding the involvement of a local Portuguese bank. I need you both to know about it.'

'Yeah, I've read a summary of your report; the usual masterpiece of caveats and obfuscation.'

'I didn't know what I was looking for and I'm not going to speculate until we have more facts. You'll appreciate that.'

Grant Douglas was the CMM's Chief Executive, an American lawyer who'd decided to make his home in Scotland whence, he was convinced, his forebears originated. Grant was very good at manipulating situations to suit his own preferences. Establishing himself in the well-paid role of CEO of a firm based in his beloved Scotland had been a masterstroke, and to be fair he'd breathed new life into an organisation that had been limping along at the tail-end of a highly competitive and sophisticated sector of the shipping industry. That, at least, was the cover, the legend. But things were not as they appeared. Things were opaque, as Grant liked to put it, though I was never sure whether he meant they were opaque by accident or design.

'Alright, but let me get this straight,' he said. 'The ship loaded military vehicles and weaponry, none of which is accurately declared on the cargo documentation. And naturally the owner's cagey as hell about it. We know they're in financial trouble and we know why. It's a question of determining our own, I mean the CMM's role going forward. I think we'd best wait this one out. I'd like to know where that cargo's headed though. And we need to discuss your own role in this too. Things have become a little blurred lately, wouldn't you say?'

My only reason for being in Leith was to visit the CMM. They provided me with a cosy little flat near the office for when I was in town, which, as far as they were concerned, was not often enough, and from my own point of view was more than often enough.

'Perhaps you'd like to clarify them for me then. But if by blurred you mean that my position as a freelance claims handler fo0r CMM is in conflict with that of field agent for the IMTF, then I'd agree,' I said, hoping to get things straight and transparent at last.

'That's what I wanted to talk about. But there's something bigger in play.'

'What's that?'

'I want Claire in on this so I don't have to repeat myself. She knows some of what's been going on but not the big picture.'

'Okay,' I said without reminding him that that was what I'd suggested five minutes beforehand. He buzzed through to her office. Her PA answered, saying she was on a call. Whilst Grant's PA, Phyllis, was a spinster in her late fifties who wore her grey hair in a bun and her glasses on a chain round her neck, Claire's was a tall, good-looking young man from Montreal whom she'd purloined from the claims department.

'Tell her to come through when she's done,' Grant ordered.

He got up from his desk and started roaming around the office. It was big enough to roam around in and he was the restless type, a tall rangy man in his sixties, silver-haired and suntanned. Today he was wearing his favoured blue shirt with white collar and cuffs, red bow tie and red braces that made him look distinctive if not distinguished, and just a little dated. Grant worked out in the basement gym every lunchtime, ate healthily and drank sparingly. In every sense he appeared a man in control. He turned back to me. I was sitting at the round conference table in the corner with a view over the Links where women were walking their dogs and kids were tearing around on scooters, bikes and skateboards.

'There're a few things you need to know,' he said without sitting down. 'Things that should have been explained a while back.'

'So why weren't they?'

He picked up his coffee, carried it over to where I was sitting with mine and finally sat down.

'Because the situation didn't warrant it. Now it does.'

'That sounds pretty opaque to me, Grant.'

'Sure. So now it's time to clarify things. Phyllis!' he shouted. Phyllis scuttled in from her adjacent office.

'Go tell Claire we need her in here now, will you.'

'Yes, sir,' Phyllis replied and left on her mission. Less

than a minute later Claire walked in holding her own mug of coffee.

'Morning, Grant,' she said, carefully placing the mug on the table. I got up and we hugged. I hadn't seen her for a few months and that was at the end of a case which had taken its toll on us both. We stood looking at each other for a moment, each of us wanting to say more than we could in Grant's presence.

'How are you?' I asked her.

'How are you, Angus?' she replied, avoiding my question. 'You've lost weight.'

'I haven't lost weight. It's just better distributed. I'm fitter.'

'Umm.'

Grant interrupted: 'Okay, when you two have finished discussing his health and wellbeing, can we get on with this? Things have changed, Gus. Been tidied up you could say – within the IMTF I mean.' He was looking out of the window now. 'Big changes. So how does this affect you? In practical day-to-day terms, not a lot. Henceforth, your formal status is that of approved unofficial agent. It's a term they use, so that should clear up any doubts you may have had.'

'Oh really?' I interrupted. I sensed Claire wincing. She knew my dealings with Grant were often fraught. 'My understanding of AUA status is that it simply provides the powers above with plausible deniability. Anyway, in case I'm missing something here, Grant, since when has my status within the IMTF been anything to do with you?'

'Whoa, just hold on, fella. Let's take this one step at a time. And remember, the intelligence services aren't organised to suit your convenience. Your role is decided by them, not by you. We're not doubting your talents but just keep that in mind. Anyhow, can we get on with this? Look, Claire, you know some of it but I want Gus in the loop now, okay? So, first off, the IMTF is being subsumed.'

'Subsumed into what?' I asked in a reasonable tone of voice.

'Amber Dove is retiring and so we're taking the opportunity to do a bit of reorganising. That's if it's approved by Clark Kent here of course.' Our relationship had always depended on a degree of mutual sarcasm. I told myself it was the best way to cope with each other's cultural differences.

'So who's taking over? Six?'

'In a manner of speaking, yes.'

'But?'

'But day-to-day executive authority will rest here.'

'With you?'

'Yes, with me. Don't sound so incredulous.'

'No, that's great. Congratulations, Grant,' I said, feigning enthusiasm. 'But beyond day-to-day, who's in charge?'

'This is all need-to-know, buddy. Can't say more than I have.'

'But is the MoD still involved or not?' I pressed.

'Let's just say they're still very much involved at committee level. Now let's move on shall we?'

'Sure,' I said. I'd ask Claire later. 'But where does that leave me? I have a business to run back in Greece, largely for the benefit of the CMM.'

'Don't tell me you don't do well out of it, and these AUA field jobs you get called in for. I thought they brightened up your day.'

I let it go. The last job had just about killed me. 'So do I report to you or to Claire?'

'Claire of course. But I'll have oversight.' Oversight or interference, I wondered.

'Shall we get on with this?' Claire interjected. 'I've read your report from Lisbon, Angus. So what's new?'

I filled them in on my conversation with Pedro Fernandes. 'So what happens now?' I concluded. 'Do you want to wait this out? I'm not sure it's relevant from the CMM's perspective.' I wanted Grant to admit at the outset that this was more than just a CMM case we were discussing.

'Okay,' said Grant. 'So this isn't about the CMM; superficially perhaps, but there are matters of strategic importance in play here as well. I'm telling you now because I'll be working closely and directly with you both on this one.'

'Why is that?'

'I know you're our ace field man, buddy, but I don't feel

I need to give a detailed explanation to you on everything I decide to do.'

'It would be helpful, Grant,' Claire said. 'Then we'll know where we all stand.'

He started prowling around the office again. Finally, he replied. 'It's straightforward enough. My people have an interest in these legacy cases you're handling, Claire. Some of their hostile takeover victims were American firms. Some were operating in the South China Sea oilfields. I'm not saying Dalmatia Shipping was one of those but we're interested in them all.'

Turning to me he said, 'I trust this explanation is satisfactory?'

'Fine with me,' I said, 'as long as we all know what each of us is supposed to be doing.'

'Sure, so keep me in the loop, okay.'

'Likewise, Grant.'

Before he could respond Claire opened her hand and produced a flash drive as if performing a conjuring trick. She handed it to Grant. 'This is the CMM file. It includes Angus's report, not this latest stuff about Banco Imperio of course.' She glanced at me before continuing. 'Grant, you understand we're going to need some kind of authorisation on this don't you. You know what I'm talking about.'

'Sure. You'll get it. I just wanted to draw you a little diagram before we get too deeply into this case. But you'll be hearing from your naval pals, don't worry.'

He looked pointedly across the table at each of us. 'Right, now all you need to know is that we're all on the same side.'

I didn't find what he was saying at all reassuring but we left it like that even though we hadn't got a proper answer from him, like who he, or now we, were really working for. But then I hadn't really expected one. People in this business didn't make a habit of disclosing their employer's names and addresses.

I went next door to Claire's office. As we chatted, I wrote a note on a scrap of paper and passed it across the desk. It said: *Tonight at 7. Conan Doyle. Leave your phones here.* She just nodded. I didn't think her office would be bugged but in light of what Grant Douglas had just been saying, I didn't want to risk speaking openly to Claire there.

CHAPTER 4

The Conan Doyle is close to the great man's birthplace at the point where Leith joins Edinburgh, and not too far from the CMM's offices. In the past, Claire and I had met at The Shore, an old waterside pub just a ten-minute walk from the office, but on our last visit we'd encountered a crowd of CMM people rowdily celebrating someone's birthday. The nature of our conversations demanded that we met somewhere discreet. I'd told her to leave her phones behind, and I'd left mine back in my flat because I was uneasy about Grant's sudden interest in the case and the possibility that he might track our whereabouts. Despite the banter and sarcasm, we both respected him. But that was in his role as boss of the CMM. It was Grant who'd been largely responsible for Claire's rapid ascent to her present position as Chief Operating Officer, and on a previous occasion he'd dug me out of a hole which, though not of my own making, had threatened to bring an abrupt end to my relationship with the CMM.

But now he'd more or less confirmed what we'd long suspected: that he was a deep cover intelligence officer working for the Americans. While he was an inactive sleeper we hadn't bothered to dig into his covert life, but now that he'd come out and announced his involvement with the IMTF and the interest of his "people", along with his intention of directing the *Dalmatia Star* case, alarm bells were ringing.

Of course, Grant knew of Claire's role in the IMTF and of my own more recent enrolment. But while he would certainly have known the details of the cases we were involved in, he had never interfered. Now, it seemed all that was changing.

As for the *Dalmatia Star*, you didn't need to be Sherlock Homes to deduce that there was a serious intelligence dimension to the case by virtue of the ship's cargo.

Claire was my case officer but I'd missed the chance to talk to her before I was cornered by Grant that morning. Now suddenly he was acting like he knew more about the case than I did.

I arrived early, ordered my pint and, glass in hand, moved around the pub slowly until I was satisfied there was no one there I knew or who looked out of place. Then I found a quiet corner, sat down and waited for Claire.

She was ten minutes late and entered in a rush, pulling off her woolly hat and shaking her dark hair loose before she spotted me. She slipped out of her coat as she came over. 'God, it's freezing out there,' she said holding her hand against my face to prove it.

'What are you having?'

'Glass of Chablis if they have it please.'

I went to the bar, ordered her wine and returned to find her with her back to the radiator. She took a sip, looking at me over the rim of the glass. At forty she was as attractive as she had been when I'd first met her fifteen years earlier: petite, with fine features, big brown eyes and lightly tanned skin. I'd sometimes wondered if she had Mediterranean blood, though her temperament did not suggest it. She was one of the calmest people I knew, but that hadn't always been so. Fifteen years ago she'd been a headstrong young case handler for the CMM who'd got herself into a dangerous situation in the Black Sea port of Poti. Operating as I did, out of Piraeus, I'd been asked by Grant to go and fetch her out. In the course of doing so we'd become lovers and despite her subsequent marriage and my own long-term involvement with a Greek girl, Claire and I had remained very close, to the point that neither of us seemed willing or able to break off our affair, something that plagued both of us with guilt. The situation had been further complicated by my getting dragged into working for the IMTF, whereby I reported to her. As I looked at her now I still didn't know how to reconcile these conflicts.

'So what's going on?' I asked, keeping my voice low.

'I haven't had a chance to bring you up to date, darling,' she began, speaking softly, the way she always did. 'So, where to start? You need to know what's happening at the IMTF. They're under fire, Angus. It looks like Six will take them over within the next month, max. This was all going on in the background when you were on that last gig in Hong Kong.'

'Don't tell me: Ben Wood was a plant, right?'

'Yes. I think we always suspected it. He was seconded to us from Six but there was a hidden agenda. Only it wasn't particularly well hidden, was it!'

'So where does that leave Amber?' Commodore Amber Dove was the head of the IMTF. She was a long-serving Royal Navy officer who'd been with the IMTF since it was spun off from Naval Intelligence into the MoD's Defence Intelligence years before. I guessed the answer before Claire said it.

'She's retired: pensioned off after that last case. I don't think her masters were too impressed by the way she wrapped it up, but they were just looking for an excuse. Six has had their eye on us for years. Amber was a scapegoat.'

'Is it a bad thing?'

'What I hear is they want to take over our cases and absorb us completely – consolidation they call it – the standard euphemism for a takeover of course. Where that leaves you and me I'm not sure, but I gather having the CMM as a cover for the IMTF's work suits the powers that be both in Vauxhall Cross and with our friends in Langley. There are plenty of precedents. Ben Wood was working for a well-known British Bank in Tehran at one point in his career. You know how they like to keep people like us hidden away.'

'To tell you the truth, I'm not too concerned for myself,' I said. 'I still feel I got dragged into this business. It wasn't exactly a career choice. What about you? Do you welcome all these developments?'

'I don't know. But after what Grant's just told us I feel I'm losing control. Why would he want to take over this case, which is pretty much what he said he was doing?'

'Because he knows something that we don't,' I said. 'Even before I told you both of my conversation with Fernandes, he knew something. Why else would he suddenly intervene?'

'And I'm the one sorting out those hostile takeover legacy cases,' she said. 'I've kept him fully informed and he's never even hinted that he wanted to get involved. So why now?'

'Perhaps we're being over-cautious,' I said without much conviction. The point of convergence between what was a potential claim governed by the CMM's rule book and something more sinister and therefore of interest to the IMTF, was an indistinct grey line. It hadn't worried me too much in the past but now things had changed. A year or so back someone had told me that Grant Douglas was a "friend". In the context of that conversation I'd taken it to mean he worked for either the CIA or some other US intelligence agency. Back then it hadn't mattered. He wasn't involved in those cases. But now here he was telling us he was running the show.

We carried on speculating as to Grant's interest and intentions as to the *Dalmatia Star*. In the end I asked, 'How do you want me to handle it?'

'In your usual masterful way, my love. I trust you, and so does Grant. He told me once you've got your own unofficial and exclusive sources of information. You dig out stuff that no one else can find. And what you don't know you guess at and usually get it right – usually. But he says you're reckless, and always complaining. I think he just feels a bit intimidated by you, that's all.'

I guess men often find it difficult to exchange compliments and Grant was no exception. Neither was I for that matter.

'I have other news,' she sighed, taking a large gulp of her wine. 'Edward and I are splitting, finally.'

'You've said that before, Claire.'

'We've handed it to the lawyers this time.' And suddenly her voice broke and I could see she was close to tears. I'd seen Claire under huge pressure. I'd watched her kill a man. I'd seen her anxious and frightened, but there'd always been that composure derived, I assumed, from an inner strength, and I'd certainly never seen her defeated. Now she seemed to sag and I wondered whether her self-belief was wavering.

'Tell me.' I reached over and held her cold hands in mine.

'It all broke after the last case when we were in Hong Kong. He's such a bloody hypocrite. He goes off with his PA all over the world attending conferences. She's always with him. I've never told you before but I had him watched on four separate occasions just to be sure.'

'Watched? Where?'

'Stockholm, Sydney, Boston, and just recently in Dubai.'

'What do you mean by watched?'

'It was over a period of years, four actually. I needed to know for sure. I didn't use our people of course. Just private agencies who'd been recommended. Same result each time. And it wasn't just his PA either. He had prostitutes to his room when he was in Sydney. Then I was looking at his phone. I hated doing that,' she said, the anguish showing on her face. 'This was just a couple of months ago. He hadn't even made the effort to hide or delete much of the stuff: calls and texts between them, and his texts to her were the last straw.'

'Did you talk it all through with him?'

'He wouldn't. Refused point blank and finally I knew what I needed to do. It was just the children that were stopping me. But the tension in the house, at meal times, even on holiday, it was getting to them too. Finally Iona told me they couldn't stand it. She said she was going to live with Granny, my mum. She's thirteen now but she wanted to discuss it with me, so we did. You know what she said? She said she was so proud of me, that she'd always love us both – her dad and me but it was better that we lived apart than be together and so unhappy.' She began crying.

'Out of the mouths of babes …'

'Exactly,' she sniffled. 'She'd discussed it with Fergus, her brother, and my mum. She's been brilliant. So when it finally did come to it, the big discussion, it actually didn't seem as bad as I'd feared. We'll make it work, the divorce I mean. We're both determined to for the sake of the kids.'

She looked up at me, tears in her eyes. 'Sorry to burden you with all this.'

'You should have told me before. I knew you weren't happy. You should have come to me.'

'I didn't want to make you feel you were under pressure. You're such an independent bastard. I didn't want you to feel you needed to look after me.'

'I love you, Claire. I don't see that as a burden.'

We sat in silence for a few minutes. I didn't want to remind her of the hypocrisy of which we were both guilty ourselves.

'I have some news too,' I said finally.

'What? You've got back with Elena.' she said gloomily.

'Don't be silly. No, I've bought a place on the island.'

'What! What sort of place?'

'It's an old olive mill, a ruin to be accurate. I've got an architect drawing up plans, and a local builder. Work's already started – a few weeks ago. I was going to keep it as a surprise, but with your news … It'll be somewhere we can go. It's got land with olive trees. And it overlooks the sea.'

It was on an island in the northern Aegean we'd visited together in the past to see an old, and recently deceased, colleague.

She laughed. 'You're mad.'

'I know,' I said. 'But I've been dreaming of this for years. And I need your input too.'

'For what?'

'Well, domestic stuff, interior design issues. You know …'

'Oh goodie, can I embroider all the cushions for you too?'

'Don't be sarcastic. It'll need a woman's touch.'

'You are such a dinosaur. But I love you and I'd love to get involved. You know that.'

'Great,' I said. 'It'll take your mind off things. And you can bring the children out for holidays.'

'Lovely, and my mum too?'

'Did I say that?'

She leaned across and kissed me.

CHAPTER 5

'Pedro Fernandes called. You must call him back straight away,' Zoe greeted me as I came into the office. Zoe enjoyed giving me instructions.

'Did he say what it was about?'

'No, otherwise I would have told you. Would you like me to call him now?'

'Yes please, Zoe.' Zoe Papadopoulos was the de facto boss around the office. We both accepted the situation because that was the only way the business could function efficiently. I spent more than half my time travelling, and the IMTF cases had placed even further demands on my time. It made sense.

Zoe was studying maritime law at Piraeus University. Her father was a wealthy shipowner but despite this, Zoe was determined to carve her own career. One day though I was sure she'd get a call from Papa demanding that she joined the family firm – a call she'd find hard to ignore. In the meantime she was my highly proficient office manager.

Pedro had some news concerning Banco Imperio. A delegation from the bank's executive board was in Macau meeting with the Export-Import Bank of China and the China Development Bank.

'Is that unusual?' I asked.

'Not of itself but apparently there are representatives from a Swiss bank there too. Several of this bank's officials also sit on the board of a holding company for one of Africa's sovereign wealth funds. I don't have names and I don't know which country or what these people are doing in Macau but I thought you should hear about it.'

'Thanks, Pedro. I'll keep it in mind. And let me know anything else you can find out on what these honourable bankers are doing there, will you?' It could be nothing but I'd learned that in this business it was worth following up any lead, however tenuous.

'Of course, my friend. By the way, the lady who took my call earlier, she is the manager of your company there?'

'Yes, Zoe. Why?'

'Well, she certainly knows how to manage you I would say. Charming too.'

'Yes, she can charm the birds from the trees, Pedro, but don't be fooled, she's relentless.'

He laughed. 'Yes, I sensed that too.'

No sooner had I finished the call than Zoe entered, trailing a young woman behind her. 'Meet Konstantina,' Zoe announced. Konstantina was a shy girl whom Zoe had hired in my absence. She was as different from Zoe as was possible and I just hoped this wasn't a case of Zoe finding some timid young thing who wouldn't pose a threat to her own authority. Konstantina was dark-haired while Zoe was blonde. She was tall and thin while Zoe was shorter with a voluptuous figure. And Zoe wasn't shy either. She never had been.

Hiring Konstantina, who was also a student of maritime law, wasn't the only change. The office had been redecorated. It looked good but I couldn't help wondering if Grant had had a hand in it since it more or less matched his own colour scheme. Or was I being paranoid? Space had been made for the new girl's desk too.

'It looks lovely, Zoe, but where are the filing cabinets? Where are the case files? The current ones I mean.'

'We went through this the last time I moved a mass of old files to the storeroom, Angus. It's all organised,' she said soothingly now, noting the panic in my voice. 'I've made more room in the storeroom too, and moving the filing cabinets there makes room for Konstantina here. We're getting busier every day, as you know.'

'So I have to walk out of the office, down the corridor and unlock the storeroom to get at my files.'

'Good exercise for you, Angus,' she retorted having, as always, the last word. It made sense of course. Everything she did made sense though that didn't mean I had to like it.

Most of our case correspondence was digitised now anyway, but documentation was another matter. Both the shipping industry and the legal profession still preferred to see cargo documentation, charterparties and other legally binding documents signed by human hand on paper to minimise the risk of fraud which was still so widespread in our business.

'And you need to be in Thessaloniki tomorrow, remember? Do you want me to book your flight?'

'Yes, not the early one though.'

She promptly ordered Konstantina to book me on the midday flight. 'Oh, and that garage in Lucerne has been on the phone. Your car's ready and they're wanting to know what to do with it. They say they can deliver it back here if you like.' I'd left my old Alfa Romeo in the hands of a specialist garage to carry out a full engine overhaul and some bodywork repairs following an IMTF case that had taken me to Switzerland.

'I bet they do. And add another thousand euros to the bill. Tell them I'll be collecting it myself next week. I need to go there anyway.'

She hesitated before leaving my office. 'Angus, that last case – the Dark Ocean thing? I thought it was closed.'

'It is, Zoe. Don't worry, this one I'm concerned with now isn't related. It's off the books and anyway you know we can't discuss these things.' Zoe liked to know everything, not just about our P&I business but my private life, my state of health and increasingly about the IMTF work I'd been involved in and which she had become an innocent victim of in a case which had nearly cost her her life and which she was now referring to. This inquisitiveness was what made her such a good deputy. Zoe didn't like anything to get past her, but I was bound by a code of secrecy on all my IMTF work.

'Just bring me up to speed on the P&I work will you?' I said, pushing a heap of files to one side. And that was what she did, in her usual breezy manner, obliging me to frequently interrupt with questions to which she always had a ready answer. It was a kind of game she liked to play and in which I was happy to join since it reassured me that she was on top of our case load – and back to her old self following the traumas she'd suffered on the Dark Ocean case.

There was a shortage claim on a cargo of Vietnamese rice discharged in Takoradi, a spurious stevedore injury case brought by an ambulance-chasing law firm on the US east coast, an old case involving a cargo that had allegedly been shipped from Turkey but had never arrived at the destination port of Algeciras, and a dozen or so more, all of them claims against Greek shipowners entered with the CMM and which we were retained to defend in order to reach the best possible outcome. Zoe gave me a summary of each case's current status and we agreed on the course of action we should take – a tactical exercise which would invariably lead to an out of court compromise settlement.

'One other thing,' said Zoe. 'You know I was supposed to spend time in the CMM office in Edinburgh. Is that still going to happen?'

'Of course it is.' It had all been arranged months ago. I'd even driven her to the airport for the early morning flight to Edinburgh. Which was when a series of harrowing events had occurred that I'd feared would change Zoe forever. I still wasn't sure she'd fully recovered but her desire to go to Leith for a six-week on-the-job training course was a good sign. 'Once Konstantina is up to speed we'll get some dates organised.'

That evening I walked back to my flat on Profitis Ilias. I'd been lucky to find this relative haven of peace and tranquillity on a hill above the chaos that was the port of Piraeus. The flat was on the top floor of a three-storey block perched on top of the hill. It had three bedrooms, one of which served as an office, and views looking east over the harbour of Micro Limano down the coast to Glyvada and Vouliagmeni. Half of the view, that to the south, took in part of the Saronic Gulf and I stood on the balcony with a beer watching the fishing boats and beyond them, inter-island ferries manoeuvring in towards the port. Beyond them lay the bigger ships at anchor – mostly tankers and bulk carriers. I was spending less and less time here and relished occasions like this when I could relax and reflect, if only for a few hours. The nights were getting cooler now and I stepped inside. One wall of the lounge was lined with books, many of which were waiting to be read. I browsed through some of them for a while then realised there was nothing in the fridge except a few beers. I was putting my jacket on to go across to the neighbouring taverna when my phone rang. It was Grant.

'Listen, Gus, I've got to go to the States for a few days so Claire will be minding the store, but when I'm back I'm sending her down to Lisbon to check out this Banco Imperio lead. Just keeping you in the loop on this one, okay?'

'I appreciate that, Grant.' I'd told Claire of Pedro's news regarding the bank's Macau meetings and suspected that it was Claire's idea, and not Grant's, that she should follow it up in Lisbon. Recently Grant had become over-sensitive about this kind of situation as he strove to impose his authority on a team that was already functioning perfectly well without him. I sympathised with him – up to a point. We chatted on for a while until Grant said he must get going. He had to meet someone for dinner.

Next day I left for Thessaloniki.

***

Greece's northern city is as different from Athens as Edinburgh is from London. Although vibrant with commerce, festivals and cultural events, it is more laid-back than the capital and its people less frenzied. It was a place I always looked forward to visiting but on this occasion I had mixed feelings. I'd come to see Sonia Babic, the widow of Luka Babic, the recently deceased master of the *Dalmatia Star*. Claire had set up the meeting through the ship's owners, Dalmatia Shipping in Rijeka. Although the family had an apartment in Croatia, Sonia Babic and their two children had moved back to her family home in Panorama, an affluent suburb overlooking the city of Thessaloniki.

It was one of those bright winter days with warmth in the sun and autumn blossom still on the trees that made me glad I lived in Greece. The house was old, dating back to the days when Thessaloniki was a thriving outpost of the Ottoman Empire and well before the ravages of the twentieth century. I walked through wrought-iron gates up the path to the front door. The garden was untidy but seemed to have everything: fruit trees, vines, flower beds and shrubs, and amongst all this, winding paths leading to hidden corners. The house itself resembled a small mansion and, like the garden, was dilapidated with plaster flaking from the walls and the paintwork around the windows bleached by the sun.

I pressed the bell push and heard it ring inside. An old lady clothed in black came to the door and ushered me in. As my eyes adjusted to the dim interior of the hall another woman appeared out of the gloom, younger, but also dressed in black.

'Mr McKinnon? I am Sonia Babic. This is my mother.' I shook Sonia's hand but the old woman departed without speaking.

'Come into our living room,' she said, turning and heading towards the back of the house. We entered a large room with a high ceiling and tall windows through which the winter sun shone, highlighting the dust on the glass.

She gestured to a chair and sat down opposite me. 'My mother is not well. But she will bring us coffee.'

Captain Babic's widow was in her mid-forties, tall with dark hair which was already turning grey. I noticed dark patches under her eyes. She looked and sounded exhausted.

'I'm sorry to trouble you now,' I said addressing her in Greek. 'I won't take up much of your time.'

Despite herself she smiled. 'That's alright. It's good to have a visitor. But perhaps we should speak English? Your Greek is good, but …'

'I know. Yes, perhaps we should.'

'Are you from Scotland? Your name?'

'My parents were Scottish. I live in Piraeus. I still visit Scotland though.'

'And you are from the ship's P&I Club. Miss Papadopoulos explained. I do know something about marine insurance. I met Luka when I was working for an agent here in Thessaloniki. My father had his own business and I worked for him. We handled the Dalmatia vessels when they called. That was twenty years ago. Luka was still second mate then.'

'Where are your children now?'

'The boys are both at school. Do you have children?'

'No,' I said. 'Tell me, Mrs Babic …'

'Sonia.'

'Sonia, I know this is hard, but was Luka under a lot of pressure? Was he depressed? Did you ever think he might take his own life?'

She looked directly at me, dignified and composed. 'Not for one second. Luka was just not that type. He was a cheerful man, full of laughter and so confident and positive about everything. I do not believe he took his life. Why? We have … we had a good marriage, and the boys – he lived for them, their future …' And with mention of her two sons the mask of composure dropped, she leaned forward with her face in her hands and sobbed.

If I'd known her better I would have moved over to comfort her, but I didn't so I sat and waited and within a few moments she regained her poise. She blew her nose and laughed, a bitter laugh. 'He was murdered. I am convinced of it. Do you know what was happening with Dalmatia Shipping? You know he had shares in the company?'

'Yes,' I said. Then I told her what I could disclose of the case.

'I understand you lifted him down?'

'Yes, that's right.'

She stared at me waiting for me to go on. When I

hesitated she said, 'You carried him to his bunk, yes? With the padre?'

'Yes. We laid him there. The padre anointed him.'

'He did not receive the sacraments?'

'No, apparently that is only for the living – the last rites. But the padre prayed for his soul. Luka was a Catholic I understand.'

'Yes. Not so devout, but you know, we can never quite renounce our faith. I am Orthodox of course. Thank you for doing that. And I would like you to thank the padre too. Is that possible?'

'Of course.'

'Then he was taken ashore on the tug, and to the morgue in Lisbon I am told. We are still awaiting the results of the post mortem.'

'That's right. And Zoe or I will keep you informed.'

Her mother came into the room carrying an ornate silver tray with a large *briki* from which she poured coffee into two heavily decorated cups.

'*Metrio* is good?'

'*Metrio* is fine thanks. Sonia, do you know of anyone who might have wished your husband harm?'

'The company was in trouble, you know that. He joined when the ship called here for fuel and stores just a few weeks ago; on her way from Trabzon. He was fine. He didn't know where they were to discharge but …'

'Did he not mention the cargo they had loaded in Trabzon?'

'Yes, second-hand trucks he said, maybe for Africa.'

'He didn't mention they were military vehicles?'

'No, not to me. But his death was reported in the media here and I received a call just yesterday from a man we used to do business with in the agency – a lawyer called Carasso.'

'Benjamin Carasso? I know him. He's done work for me up here.'

'Yes, he told me so when I said you were coming to visit me. He said he would be pleased to meet with you.'

'So what did he say?'

'Only that he had information that may be of interest to you.'

'He didn't tell you what it was?'

'I told him I didn't want to know. I rely on you to find out what happened to my Luka. It happened when the ship was in international waters and you know what that means.'

'Yes, jurisdiction lies with the flag state.'

'Exactly, some little island in the South Pacific that's about to disappear under the sea. The Portuguese aren't interested either. You find out for me, Mr McKinnon. Please.'

Before I could respond there was a commotion in the hall and two small boys came rushing into the room shouting at each other. Their mother rose to calm them and introduced each of them to me in turn: 'Luka and Nicola. They keep me sane,' she said.

As I was leaving she picked up a framed family photo from a table in the hall and showed it to me. It showed all four of them in the sea, laughing and fooling around. Both boys were clinging onto their father's back. 'That was taken three months ago,' she said before seeing me to the door.

CHAPTER 6

'You alreet the noo, laddie?' Benny Carasso's attempt at a Scottish accent, which he affected whenever we met, sounded bizarre considering he was a Sephardic Jew from Thessaloniki who'd spent half his life in New York. And despite the circumstances of our meeting, it made me laugh as it always did, not least because I had difficulty speaking Scots myself.

Benny was old, maybe eighty, but his mind was sharp. He was bent and walked with a silver-topped ebony cane which was now propped against the table we sat at. What was left of his hair was wispy and white. He wore a black suit with a waistcoat. His appearance reminded me of some character from an old black and white movie. But Benny was no cardboard cut-out and what kept him young in mind, body and soul was his unfailing sense of humour, often at others' expense though never meant unkindly.

'I'm fine, Benny. Keeping well yourself? How's the leg?' We were sitting in a little taverna in the Modiano Market, the biggest covered market in the city. Mostly it's crammed with food stores selling spices, cheese, fish, meat and delicatessen products. Walk through the place and you can feel the spirit and scents of the old city. The whole area evokes its Jewish past. Ninety-six percent of Thessaloniki's Jewish population perished in the Holocaust, most of them transported direct by rail to the Nazi death camps. Many of the buildings around us had once been the mansions of wealthy Jewish families. Despite their elegant and well cared-for façades it wasn't hard to imagine ghosts of the past roaming their halls at night. Benny's family had been lucky – or smart. They'd been descendants of the Sephardic diaspora that had fled from Spain in the late fifteenth century following the *Reconquista*. But as storm clouds gathered over Europe in the late 1930s, they had abandoned this city that had been home to the family for over five hundred years and settled in New York.

'Still attached to my hip last time I looked. Never mind that, Angus my boy, I want to talk about the *Dalmatia Star* and poor Luka Babic. I'm close to the family you know.' He reached into an ancient leather bag that needed re-stitching round the seams and pulled out a folder.

'Take a look at these.'

I flicked through the sheaf of papers, then studied them more carefully as I realised the story they were telling. The one that caught my eye was a letter of credit guaranteeing payment for the *Dalmatia Star*'s Trabzon cargo.

'Where did you get these, Benny?'

He tapped the side of his nose. 'You know better than to ask, eh?'

The goods were listed as military equipment, the beneficiary as Trabzon Logistics AS and the buyer as a company in Switzerland called West Africa Development Factoring, an unfamiliar name to me. But it was the issuing bank's name that caught my attention. Credit Sud of Zurich was one of several banks owned by the Gertch family who had made their fortunes after the war allegedly laundering Nazi loot for members of the ODESSA, the organisation set up to help SS officers escape justice by establishing themselves mostly in South America but in North Africa too. In the Cold War years the Credit Sud continued its nefarious activities, laundering gold looted by the Japanese in the war for the benefit of the United States in its fight against the growing tide of Communism. Except the Gertch brothers siphoned off millions not just for themselves but, on instructions from the CIA, for payments to KGB agents in return for Soviet state and military intelligence secrets.

The receiving bank was just as interesting, though less of a surprise: Banco Imperio of Lisbon. The letter of credit showed a clear link between the two banks and the military cargo on board the *Dalmatia Star*. What it didn't show was the cargo's destination.

'A nexus?' he asked.

'Looks like it. Thanks, Benny. I'm not asking you to reveal your sources, but if you had to guess whether there was a state player behind this, who would you choose?'

He rubbed his chin and leaned forward. 'Well, you got four choices haven't you. You got the Portuguese trying to bring about a regime change in one of its former colonies, which would certainly point to Africa. You got the Chinese, who might be changing their modus operandi from economic to military intervention – again in Africa. Then the Russkies, who we know are getting more active by the day selling arms and training the military in several African states.'

'And number four?'

'It's not impossible is it. Look at Laos, Nicaragua, Panama, Angola and the rest.'

'A CIA black op?' I said. 'It's possible I suppose. There are several African coastal states with offshore energy reserves that Big Oil are already heavily invested in.'

Benny was warming to his theory: 'So why not?' he said. 'Uncle Sam might want to encourage a regime change somewhere if they feel the local government isn't playing ball with its strategic interests. Covertly of course.'

Of course.

CHAPTER 7

'Nice work, Matteo,' I said as I walked round the car. My old Alfa Romeo had been transformed by Matteo's workshop on the outskirts of Lucerne. They'd fitted it with a 185 horsepower Twin Spark engine to replace the original Nord. Then they'd tweaked the new engine, the brakes and the suspension. They'd repaired and resprayed the body in its original racing green and replaced the worn plastic seats with tan leather ones. It was still an old car, not a concours classic but the facelift had breathed new life into my treasured possession.

'How much?' I asked him. The workshop itself was something to behold: spotlessly clean and every tool in its place around the walls. I spotted a 1950s Maserati and two old Mercedes from the same era, all in varying states of renovation.

'Don't ask me. I will let you know. There is no hurry to pay the balance; it was a privilege to work on such a car.'

I didn't press him. I'd put down a hefty deposit already

and was in no hurry to see how much more he wanted. I drove off, enjoying getting used to the different feel that the car had been given.

I'd flown from Thessaloniki to Zurich to follow up on what I'd learned from Pedro and Benny Carasso, and to renew an acquaintance. Only I wasn't sure where to find her.

First I headed for Helmut Gertch's estate on the northern shores of the lake just a few miles east of Lucerne, near the district of Meggen. Gertch had departed this life right in front of me and in dramatic style not so long ago. The estate was now on the market. But today it was his personal nurse and companion I wanted to see. Zoe had been unable to track her down and I was having no luck either. The gates to the estate were closed and no one was answering the bell. I contemplated climbing over as I had on that previous occasion but instead returned to town and the office of the estate agent who was handling the sale. They told me Gudrun Sandmeier had moved to Burgenstock and was working in a hotel there. So I drove round the lake as the rain turned to sleet and white horses reared up from its grey waters. One day, I told myself, I'd visit Switzerland when the weather was warm and sunny.

When I got to the hotel I was told Gudrun had left a few weeks earlier.

'Do you know where she went?' I asked the receptionist, who was eyeing me with suspicion. 'Where is her home?'

'I'm afraid she didn't leave a forwarding address.'

'I need to see her urgently. Is there anything you can do to help me find her? She helped me once,' I added hoping it might make a difference.

The girl sighed. 'I have a number for her somewhere,' she said opening a drawer behind the counter. 'Here.' She handed me a scrap of paper. 'She told me not to give this out but I guess it doesn't do any harm to call her, then she can decide if she wants to see you or not.'

I wrote the number down, handed the note back and thanked her, then stepped outside and called from the lakeside. Looking across from this southern shore, north towards Meggen, I was reminded of that long day and the night that followed when violent death had visited the Gertch home. I shuddered and pulled my collar up against the driving sleet. I was about to give up on the call when a voice answered. '*Gruetzi wohl?*'

'Gudrun? It's Angus McKinnon, remember me?'

There was a long pause. 'What do you want?'

'Can we meet? It's about the Credit Sud, the Gertch bank in Zurich. I have some questions.'

Another pause. Then: 'I don't want anything to do with those people.'

'Gudrun, this is important to me but it needn't worry you. It's a case I'm working on.'

'Are you alone? Where are you?'

'Yes, I'm alone. I'm in Burgenstock.'

'What is it you want to know?'

'Nothing that will be of any risk to you, I promise. I just need to get in touch with the bank. I will explain if we can meet.'

'I see. Alright then, you know Beckenried? I am very close. Come to the Hotel Nidwaldnerhof. It's on the lake. I will be in the restaurant there in half an hour's time.'

When I got to the hotel she was sitting in a corner of the empty dining room, a lonely figure gazing out over the windswept waters. Gudrun Sandmeier looked older than when I'd last seen her not that long ago. That is to say she looked like a dowdy, careworn seventy-year-old as opposed to a brusque, well-groomed sixty-year-old. Her actual age must have been somewhere in between.

'Hello, Gudrun.'

She jumped as I woke her from whatever daydream she'd been having. 'Mr McKinnon. This is a surprise.' She spoke slowly, adjusting to English, which she spoke fluently but with a strong *Schweizerdeutsch* accent. 'Shall I order you coffee?' She hailed the young waitress who was hovering on the other side of the room.

'I'm sorry to intrude on your privacy like this,' I said, sitting down opposite her. 'Are you hiding? At the hotel they were reluctant to give me your number.'

The girl came over to take our order.

'After Herr Gertch's death people came: people from his family banking business. They asked so many questions. They wanted me to sign so many papers, and to keep my mouth shut. They threatened me with legal action – I had signed a non-disclosure agreement - but psychologically too. I was afraid. They said I should be afraid. So I agreed to sign their papers. Then I came here. You found me and I'm sure they could if they wished. I didn't want to see you but it was you and your Japanese friend who put an end to that dreadful business.' She shuddered. 'Oh, how horrible that was.'

'Yes, it was. But I appreciate what you did for me that day.'

'How is your head?' she asked. And at last she smiled. 'I thought you would not wake up after they hit you like that.'

'I'm fine, thanks to your treatment.'

'I was a registered intensive care nurse you know, before Herr Gertch employed me.'

'And now? Are you managing?'

'Yes, I manage. I miss my work. Retirement didn't suit me so I took work in the hotel where you called from but that didn't suit me either.' She laughed bitterly as if she felt her life had been ruined by what had happened. 'Anyway, what is it you need to know?'

'Gudrun, do you have any friends at the bank, Credit Sud I mean?'

'No, no.' She paused before remembering. 'Oh, but I

know the woman Herr Gertch dealt with there. She used to come to the house sometimes and I would serve her tea. She was a good woman. Herr Gertch thought so too. We both liked her.'

'Are you in touch with her still?'

'No, no, but why do you ask?'

I showed her the letter of credit and told her what I wanted.

'That is all?'

'Yes. I don't want to make things difficult for her, or for you.'

'Tell me why you want to know these things. What is this case of yours?'

'I'm afraid I can't tell you more than I already have.'

'Are you a spy, Mr McKinnon?'

'No, just an insurance investigator. And I'm on the side of the angels, I promise.'

She looked at me sceptically, but after a while said, 'I will let you know what I can find out. Give me your telephone number please.'

'Better if I call you. I'll be on the move.'

'Very well, if you prefer.'

We drank our coffee. 'Do you manage? Financially I mean.'

'Oh yes. I do not need to work. Herr Gertch was very generous. He provided for me well.'

'I'm glad.'

'He was not a bad man, Mr McKinnon. Perhaps his father and his uncles did some bad things after the war, but Herr Gertch himself? No, he was a good man, not a strong man but not a bad man.'

I offered her a lift but she said she lived nearby and would walk.

'In this?' I said looking out over the water. I remembered hiding in the woods nearby observing the comings and goings at the Gertch house across the lake.

'Oh, I don't mind this stormy weather,' she said.

I finished my coffee and left her there, hoping I'd at least relieved some of the monotony in her life. Or had I just given her one more thing to worry about?

***

Before beginning the long drive back to Greece I found a small hotel for the night outside Lugano. I called Claire, then Zoe and had a quiet dinner down the road from the hotel. The *raclette* was prepared and served with Swiss precision. I washed it down with a bottle of Fendant and turned in early.

Next morning I left at eight and headed north then east, skirting round Lake Como to avoid Milan. From there I would continue eastwards to Venice, catch a ferry down the Adriatic to Igoumenitsa and head down to Athens from there.

I was driving through the Valtellina past Berbenno when they came after me. The winter sun was warmer here and vineyards stretched either side of the road as a reminder that I was moving away from the chill of the Alps. The new audio system Matteo had fitted was playing Puccini. For once I was in no hurry. I had the window down, the scenery was fabulous and I was feeling good about the way the Alfa was handling.

The big Audi SUV appeared in the rear-view mirror. I signalled for him to pass once we reached a straight stretch of road. The car drew alongside. It was black: black paintwork, black wheels and blacked-out windows. He didn't pass but instead stayed parallel. I looked across to signal him but he stayed where he was. Did he want to race? That happened sometimes in Greece but here? I picked up my speed. Still he was there. Ahead I could see off to my right that the road ran alongside the river. The bank was steep with only a low wall of white-painted breezeblocks serving as a barrier. Beyond, I caught a glimpse of the rapids as the river narrowed into a gorge. Further down the road I could see the entrance to a tunnel. I braked but still he stayed alongside. I could pull up or else face plunging down the bank into the river, or into the wall of the tunnel. Before I could process these disagreeable alternatives, they were decided for me. The SUV suddenly turned and slammed into the side of the Alfa. I turned the wheel hard left towards him in response but an Audi Q7 is twice the size and weight of the Alfa. There was the sound of metal grinding on metal but my manoeuvre had no other effect beyond that. I was going to be driven off the road.

I braked sharply but it was too late. I was forced off the road, smashed through the breezeblocks and down the bank. The last thing I remember was seeing the Audi accelerating away as I plunged over the edge.

How long I lay in the car before regaining consciousness I'm not sure. Not long. I found myself suspended upside down by the seatbelt but my head was jammed against the roof, twisting it to one side. My neck hurt like hell and I remember thinking that might not be a bad sign. The engine had stopped running and I could hear the sound of the river. I could smell petrol too. Then I heard voices.

In the end someone managed to release my seatbelt and two men dragged me out through the open window. The doors were too buckled to open.

They were farm labourers by their appearance. They spoke rapidly to each other in the way men who work together do. I didn't understand a word of what they were saying. After I'd been laid beside the river I began to take stock of my condition. I moved my legs first, then my arms, which was a mistake. From the pain that shot through my left shoulder I was sure it was broken. And my ribs on that side hurt when I breathed. Everything else seemed to be working, but I didn't risk sitting up. The men stayed with me. They continued to talk in rapid Italian. It was unclear whether they were trying to offer me reassurance or just discussing the extraordinary vagaries of life, but after a while I heard the sound of an ambulance's siren.

I turned my head slowly to look at the car, ignoring the shooting pain in my neck. It was lying on its roof. Steam was blowing out from the radiator. I wondered how many times it had rolled before coming to rest on the stony river bank. The Quadrifoglio badge on the front wing was scratched and smeared in mud. Alfa Romeo had originally introduced the four-leaf clover as a symbol of good luck for their racers back in the 1920s. Mine hadn't lasted long. God only knew what damage had been done. It was probably a write-off. I looked away.

CHAPTER 8

As it turned out I did get lucky, even if the car didn't. The X-ray at the local hospital revealed a dislocated shoulder, which the young doctor cheerfully popped back into its socket applying what he informed me was the Kocher Method: a series of adduction and abduction manoeuvres. I cried out with the sudden intense pain but felt immediate relief after it had been done. In addition I had pulled a muscle in my neck and cracked three ribs. He gave me painkillers and said I should try to breathe normally and avoid coughing.

'You were lucky not to have broken your neck,' he said as he saw me rubbing it. 'I would like you to rest here overnight so we may keep an eye on you.'

I was considering the pain in my neck and the manipulations he'd carried out to my shoulder when a question came into my mind. 'Tell me, Doctor, when a man is hanged, does he suffocate to death or is it a broken neck that kills him?'

He looked at me curiously. 'You're not thinking of trying it I hope.'

'No, but someone I knew of did hang himself recently. I wondered whether he'd suffered or whether it was very sudden.'

'This is an interesting subject but you should be resting, not worrying about such things.'

'Humour me.'

'What? Well, we do see such cases in Italy of course, as anywhere, and when I was studying it was something we did examine. So, without getting too technical,' he said, warming to the subject, 'the best way, if you can call it that, is for the neck to be broken. But it is not so easy. It all depends on two factors you see: the drop and the position of the noose around the neck. If the drop is not long enough then the person will strangle himself and choke to death. Not ideal. But if the drop is too long, then his head may well come off, which is messy of course and perhaps not how he would wish to be found. Also the weight of the person must be taken into account. It is a matter of velocity you see.'

'Yes, I see,' I said still rubbing my neck. 'Do you think a drop of half a metre would be sufficient to break his neck?'

'No. I would not have thought so, unless he was very heavy indeed.'

'And the second factor?'

'Again, the correct way, if you like to put it this way, is to place the noose under the ear. Here,' he said pointing to the spot. 'Snap go two critical vertebrae. Ideal. But you would need to know about these things to master the technique. The hangmen of old certainly did.'

'Tell me one more thing. If he had got the drop wrong and choked to death, would this be evident from … from his features?'

'His face would most likely show it, yes. As I have said, a low hanging is more likely to lead to asphyxia which would quite probably cause facial congestion or distortion and a protruding tongue which might go dark, a blue or purple colour.'

'What if the knot had been at the back of his head?'

'You ask many questions,' he laughed. 'But putting it at the back of the neck would almost certainly cause him to strangle.'

'Thanks, Doc. That's been a helpful lesson.'

'You will be alright, my friend. Get some rest now and we will discharge you in the morning.'

I sat in the little ward they gave me pondering over what he had told me. The drop between Babic's feet and the floor had certainly been no more than half a metre, neither was he a heavy man by any measure, yet his face had shown no sign of either congestion or distortion, and his tongue had not been protruding. Also, his head had hung forward and not to one side. The knot had definitely been positioned at the back of his head yet the doctor had said that would not break his neck but more likely lead to asphyxiation by strangulation. And I had the photos as evidence to support much of this. My impressions from meeting Sonia Babic and the overall questions as to the legality of the voyage, the ship's cargo and destination plus the delay in the production of a post-mortem report from Lisbon, were leading me to believe the captain had not taken his own life. Someone else had, and they'd broken his neck before stringing him up.

***

The ambulance crew had thoughtfully retrieved my jacket, overnight bag and phone from the car and the next morning I called my insurance broker in Athens, who made arrangements for the nearest garage to take the car away. As I put the phone back in my pocket it came to me: it was the phone – that was how they'd known where to find me on the road. I'd been obsessively replacing it with cheap burner phones on advice from the IMTF to avoid the risk of being tracked or listened in on, but that hadn't helped me this time. Why not? I remembered an article I'd read recently about electronic surveillance devices. They would have used a Stingray, which in effect is a portable cell phone tower that sends out signals to get a phone, mine in this case, to connect to it. Phones are programmed to connect with whichever nearby tower offers the best signal. When the phone and the Stingray connect, and the signal strength is determined from enough locations, the Stingray centralises the phone and is able to find it. The signals the Stingray send are far stronger than those coming from surrounding towers. So all phones in the vicinity connect to the Stingray without the owner's knowledge, enabling a particular phone to be tracked. I couldn't be sure but it must have been a Stingray or some similar device. And that meant they were still watching me.

There was a payphone in the hospital reception hall. I phoned Gudrun's number and she picked up straightaway. I asked her what news she had from her friend at Credit Sud.

'I have the information you want, Mr McKinnon,' she said in a conspiratorial whisper. 'The company, WADF – West Africa Development Factoring, that is – is a client of Credit Sud. It seems to be, how do you say, an umbrella, a holding company for several offshore companies which are used to invest the sovereign wealth of Kazunda, that country in West Africa you know, with the oil?'

'That's interesting, Gudrun. Did you find out who runs WADF?'

'Well, there are several directors who are non-executive and resident in Kazunda, but the executive director in Zurich is called Jawad Mendesa. This is all she could tell me. Does it help?'

'That's a big help, Gudrun. Thanks.'

'You are most welcome. And you know where to find me now if you need anything else.'

Kazunda. I knew little about the place except it had once been a Portuguese colony and was now rich in oil. The reserves were all offshore. The Americans were operating the oilfield and buying most of the production as crude for themselves, making Kazunda one of the richest states in Africa. Which was why they'd set up a sovereign wealth fund. I wondered how much of the wealth ended up benefiting the citizens of Kazunda.

Next I tried to get hold of Claire in Lisbon, this time using a burner to call her on the latest number she'd been assigned. When I got no response I tried Grant, with the same result. This kind of situation was just one reason why I preferred operating independently. Teaming up with others inevitably slowed things down and now I found myself working with, and supposedly reporting to, two case handlers.

I was about to switch off my phone and bin it when Grant called back.

'What gives with you? Still enjoying your grand tour of Europe in that old wreck of yours?'

I told him about the hit squad and how I thought they'd found me. And of what I'd learned from Gudrun Sandmeier.

'Grant, can you get a message to Claire? Tell her what's happened and tell her to take precautions.'

'Sure. She's overdue in her reporting schedule but that's not unusual for her.'

'Listen, Grant. I don't know what the reporting protocols are nowadays but there must be someone down there, either Six or your people, who can find her.' I'd learned that Grant wasn't disposed to sharing this kind of information unless pressed.

'Relax will you. I'll get hold of her, don't worry.'

'I am worried. I was nearly killed. And I'm not sure Claire is alert to the Stingray threat.'

'Course she is. She's supposed to be anyway.'

'Yes, so was I.'

'Okay, leave it with me, Gus. But who the hell did this?'

'I don't know – yet.'

'What's your plan now?'

'I was going to Zurich.'

'To see these West Africa Development people? Is that wise?'

'I'll let you know when I've seen them.'

There was a pause on the line then Grant said: 'Why don't you just head for Lisbon now, Gus? I'd feel happier if you were down there after what just happened to you.'

For once I agreed with him. Before leaving the hospital I asked the reception nurse to call a taxi to take me back to Berbenno. I switched off the phone, took out the SIM card and dumped both separately. And I made a mental note to find out more about Stingray – and how to deflect it.

Once in the cab I told the driver to head in the opposite direction, to Bergamo instead. 'I'm going to lie down,' I said.

'I'm not feeling well,' which seemed a reasonable remark coming from someone who had just left hospital. Whether the black Audi was still lurking about I couldn't tell but I'd done what I could to evade the bastards.

The cab took me to Bergamo's railway station from where I tried calling Claire again but she wasn't picking up, so I left a voicemail telling her what had happened and warning her to watch her back. Then I sat down with a coffee to think. Grant was right. What could I really achieve in Zurich? Their banks were the most secretive in the world, so gaining further access to the activities of Credit Sud was a long shot. Jawad Mendesa was who I needed to see, but for what? Was I going to walk in and ask him what he was planning to do with a ship full of military equipment? And what if he wasn't there?

Someone had tried to kill me, or at least give me a bad fright. Who? I couldn't answer that. It was tempting to assume it had something to do with the *Dalmatia Star* case but I'd learned a long time ago that making assumption was plain foolhardy. It had always struck me as an apt warning to investigators like me. And I wasn't about to jump to conclusions now. Over the past few years I had made enemies. I could count half a dozen or more dangerous men who had reason to want me dead, and had the means to make it happen.

So not for the first time, the P&I insurance dimension

of this case had been usurped by a shady geopolitical agenda. And not for the first time, I'd found myself involved against my better judgement. And once again I was plagued by self-doubt.

The death of Luka Babic had prompted the CMM's involvement, firstly because it could lead to claims for compensation and secondly because the ship's owners, of whom Babic was one, were tied up in a complex legal action over a hostile takeover – a legacy case which Claire had already been handling for some months.

The focus had shifted to the ship's cargo, whose legality was also of interest to the CMM, but it seemed of even greater interest to the intelligence community in the form of the IMTF, itself the subject of what appeared to be a coup by Britain's Secret Intelligence Service, MI6. Then there was Grant Douglas, who said he was now the case officer, but reporting to where? Vauxhall Cross, London or Langley, Virginia?

And now, I reasoned, the interest shown by these spook agencies in the *Dalmatia Star*'s cargo, suggested an impending coup d'état in the African state of Kazunda, a part of the world where coups were the time-honoured means of effecting a change of government. If Kazunda's offshore oil reserves were what I'd heard, then no wonder there was interest. And if the Americans were so heavily involved in extracting those reserves, then did that explain Grant's sudden involvement on behalf of the CIA?

Now what? Claire was pursuing the case from the Lisbon end and she was right: Lisbon was where the answers lay. I phoned Zoe and told her to get me on the next flight from Milan.

CHAPTER 9

When I emerged through Lisbon Customs I was surprised to see a man holding a sign with my name on it. So much for the covert arrival I'd hoped for.

'Who are you?' I asked him.

'Rupert Summers from the embassy. Are you McKinnon? May I see your passport?'

He looked like a Rupert Summers from the embassy. I showed it to him. 'Why the reception committee?'

'Come with me would you? I've got some bad news I'm afraid. We'll talk in the car.'

I walked with him outside to where a grey Citroën was waiting at the kerb. I put my bag in the boot and got into the back with him.

'So what's this about?' I asked as the car pulled away.

'I'm afraid your colleague, Claire Scott, has been involved in an accident.'

I took a deep breath but my heart was racing. I turned to face him. 'Go on.'

'She was in a taxi last night travelling on the coast road. The police aren't sure what happened but the car ran off the road and overturned. It landed on its roof on a beach. It had gone over a low cliff. The driver was killed. Miss Scott is in hospital.'

'What's her condition?'

'Critical. She's on life support. She's had scans revealing multiple fractures and,' he hesitated, 'head injuries.'

'Christ,' I breathed. They'd pulled the same hit job on her.

'Her next of kin has been contacted – her husband. He wanted her returned by air ambulance to Scotland immediately, but the hospital has said that would be too risky. She's fighting for her life.'

'Where is she now?'

'The Hospital da Luz, here in Lisbon.'

'Take me there will you?'

'We're on our way.'

As we headed west, he told me what else he knew: that the police had been called to the scene of an accident at 10.45 the previous evening; that there appeared to be no other vehicle involved; that the driver was already dead at the scene; and that the sole passenger, a woman, had been attended to by medics from the ambulance and transferred to the Accident and Emergency unit at the Hospital da Luz.

The journey took less than twenty minutes and I didn't

remember a thing about it. Summers accompanied me into the pristine interior of the hospital where he'd arranged an appointment with Claire's attending physician. At Reception we were directed to a private room and after five minutes the doctor arrived.

'How do you do?' she extended her hand. 'I am Doctor Sanches, Jacinta Sanches. I have received authority from your embassy to share all matters relating to this case with you. Shall we sit here and I will tell you about your colleague's injuries?'

She was a slight, dark-haired woman in her fifties. Her white coat was a size too big for her but her manner was professional and commanded attention.

'I'll wait at Reception,' Summers said and left us.

'May I see her?'

She hesitated. 'Yes, you may, but she is in a fragile state, and she is still unconscious. Let me tell you her condition first. The head injury is our main concern. There are diffuse contusions. We have placed her on a ventilator to make sure that oxygen delivery to the brain is optimal; also to lower carbon dioxide, which serves to reduce intracranial pressure. This helps to make more space in case the brain swells in response to the injury, you understand. The scan indicates that there is only diffuse bruising and no blood clotting. But we must be sure. If there is a clot then she will need surgery to evacuate it. So we will repeat the scan as necessary, to be absolutely sure.'

I'd got my own breathing and heart rate under control but a dull anxiety had replaced it, settling somewhere in my gut.

'It could be several days before she wakes up and we can take her off the ventilator and remove the endotracheal tube. After we do so she will need observation for some further days or weeks. Are you sure I cannot order you a coffee, or water perhaps?'

'I'm sure, thanks.'

'There are other injuries. She has several broken ribs, one of which has punctured her left lung,' she continued. 'So we have inserted a drain into the lung for a few days to let the air out. This we are not so concerned about but it is one reason why we do not want to put a patient with such injuries on an aircraft. The low cabin pressure can make any air spaces expand, which can be fatal. So it is best to keep her here.

'There is more I'm afraid. Her left femur suffered a compound fracture. The bone came through the skin and there was considerable loss of blood. We have given her several transfusions. The fracture will need to be repaired surgically. And as you may know, compound fractures can easily become infected. The bone is not protected by skin, which means weeks of intravenous antibiotics. Bone infections are very difficult to treat. So you see, she will not be able to leave here for some time.

'I know this is a lot to take in but there is some good news.' I was beginning to doubt it. 'Besides the punctured lung there is no sign of damage to her internal organs aside from some bruising.'

'Will there be any long-term effects from the brain injury?'

'This I cannot say. Time will tell and we will know more once she regains consciousness. There will be a period of rehabilitation, of quite intense physical therapy. We must wait and see.'

'And how soon can she be returned to Scotland do you think?'

'Again, let us wait and see.'

'Can I see her now, Doctor?'

'Of course. Come with me.'

We walked down corridors and through a number of swing doors. A nurse was in attendance as we entered the private ward. The doctor spoke to her briefly. The nurse left and the doctor examined the ventilator monitor screen. 'We should be able to put her onto spontaneous breathing within the next twenty-four hours. Regulating it is more of a precaution, you understand.'

I stared down at Claire. Tubes led from the ventilator to her nose and mouth regulating her breathing. Her dark hair on the white pillow accentuated the pallor of her skin. The tubes and the steady yet unnatural rhythmic sound of her assisted breathing made her seem all the more defenceless. The lower half of her body was covered by a kind of tent. I must have stood there for several minutes before the doctor touched my arm. 'Let us leave her now.'

Summers was waiting for us at Reception. 'Are you alright? You look like you've seen a ghost.'

'I'm okay, but I'm concerned for her safety. Can you get some kind of security detail organised here?' I said, including the doctor in my question.

'I'll organise something. Don't worry.'

'Is that going to be alright with you, Doctor?'

'Yes, of course, if it is necessary.'

'It is,' I said, then turning to Summers: 'I want it set up within the next hour. Can you fix that? Then I'd like to see the crash site.'

CHAPTER 10

The N247 threads its way from Cascais to Sintra following the coast for the first ten kilometres or so before branching inland. The sight of the Atlantic Ocean breaking against the rugged coastline is spectacular, but I wasn't looking at the view. Beneath me lay a car, a black Mercedes taxi with a green roof. It was clear from the state of it that it had rolled over several times before coming to rest upside down on the rocks below the road.

I looked down at the waves rushing into the car through an open rear door. The tide was rising and threatened to fill the interior. I stepped back and looked up the road. There were black skid marks clearly visible where the car had braked heavily, yet there was no bend ahead.

'The police reckon he braked to avoid an oncoming car that was overtaking,' said Summers. 'That would make sense to me. Look, he's driving along southbound on the right, okay? Something travelling north moves out ahead to overtake another vehicle. Taxi swerves to avoid him and sails over the edge. The other cars just carry on, not wanting to get involved.'

I just nodded. I wasn't going to upset his convenient theory of what might have happened by sharing my own thoughts with him. If Summers reckoned it was an accident maybe the police would draw the same conclusion, which wouldn't necessarily be a bad thing. I wasn't sure whether I wanted the local constabulary asking questions that might hinder my own investigation as to who had done this.

'I'm going down to take a look,' I said.

'You'll get wet.'

I ducked under the police accident tapes and clambered down, careful not to lose my footing on the slippery rocks. I reached the car and moved round to the seaward side where the rear door was open to the elements. I peered inside. Despite the cleaning effect of the sea rushing in and out, there were still blood stains visible on the upholstery, both front and back. I tried to imagine what it would have been like for her: that second of realisation as the car left the road and crashed down the cliff; then merciful loss of consciousness, or so I hoped.

I began to examine the car's bodywork. The side panels had been heavily scraped and dented as it had rolled. I moved around the wreck, examining it closely, but could see no sign of what I was looking for: evidence of another vehicle having forced the taxi off the road. I made my way back up to the road where Summers was waiting. 'How long before they remove it?'

'Tomorrow morning they've said.'

I stood there for a while hoping to gain some further insight into what had happened but all I could think of was Claire lying there bleeding in the darkness as the ocean washed around her.

We drove back to Lisbon to a hotel that Summers had found for me in the Baixa district. He made a couple of calls on his phone. 'We've got the security boys there now, at the door to her ward and outside patrolling the site. Four in all, on twenty-four hour duty relieved by another team every six hours.'

'Thanks for that.'

'Are you going to be alright?'

'I'm fine. Let's keep in touch.'

'You know where to find me,' he said, handing me a card. I didn't distrust Summers, I just didn't want to get caught up with embassy protocols and bureaucracy even if he was one of the resident spooks.

I left the hotel and walked round the corner to a pay-phone I'd spotted. First I called Grant. He already had an outline of what had happened from the embassy and there wasn't much I wanted to add at this point despite his persistent questioning. I told him I'd report fully once I'd made some progress. Then I called Pedro and asked him to meet me and bring a couple of burner phones with local SIM cards from different telecom providers.

It was dark by the time he came into the bar I'd found in a back street down near the Tejo. It wasn't as elegant as some in the area, but it was discreet.

'Scotch?'

'Thanks.'

I ordered then gave him a full account of what had happened to Claire, and of my own encounter in Lombardy.

'What now?'

I took a long pull on the whisky. 'I'll get these bastards, Pedro.'

'Sure you will. But what's your plan?' Plan? I could barely think straight, never mind plan.

'Do you even know who they are? Either way they'll be after you again sooner or later.'

'I need to lie low, Pedro. Is there somewhere you know where I can hole up?'

He thought about it for a moment. 'I have somewhere in mind. It's not a luxury penthouse but if you keep your head down you should be safe there.' Then he leaned forward: 'Your own people must have a safe house here, no?'

'I'm sure they do, but they didn't do much to protect Claire Scott did they? I want to talk to Lopes, the ship's agent. Can you fix a meeting – somewhere quiet?'

'I don't think that's a good idea, Angus. I told you before, he cannot be trusted and the bank is a powerful organisation here, with a past and present they are keen to hide. Lopes might be useful in telling you more about the *Dalmatia Star* but you can be sure your interest in the ship will be conveyed back to the bank.'

He was probably right although my instinct was to go after Banco Imperio. I knew I was missing something. There were unanswered questions and whatever Claire had discovered, she was in no position to tell me about it now.

But Pedro was viewing things from a wider perspective. And he was thinking more rationally than I was at that moment.

'No,' he said. 'Look what happened: first to you then to her. Right now ask yourself what is your objective here. What is it you are hoping to achieve?'

'I need to find out all about your former colony of Kazunda and a man called Jawad Mendesa.' I told him what I'd learned already including the connection between Mendesa and the Banco Imperio via WADF and Credit Sud.

'Then there is someone else you should meet if you wish to pursue the Kazunda connection. Her name is Mariana Da Cunha. She is a *retornado*.'

'Who or what is a *retornado*, Pedro?'

'They are the so-called "returned": those Portuguese who came back from our former colonies in the mid-seventies and after, mostly from Africa but from Timor too. They fled during the independence wars and the decolonisation process. Many, like Mariana, were born there: Angola, Mozambique, Guinea Bissau and in her case, Kazunda. And many were destitute when they came to Portugal. So it is sometimes seen as a derogatory term but often these people are well educated and have adjusted well to life in Portugal, others not so well.

'Mariana was born in what is now Kazunda. She was fourteen or so I believe when the family fled. Her father and brother were killed in the fighting that followed independence. Mariana and her mother escaped.'

'That's interesting, but why should I meet her in particular?'

'She is an old friend of my wife. We know her well. She harbours a deep resentment towards those responsible for the death of her father and brother, and for ruining a country she saw as her homeland. I will not mention this case of course, but I could mention your interest in Kazunda to her. I know she is involved with other Kazundan *retornados*. I do not know exactly what their plans are but she is very interested in the current unrest there.'

'Alright, Pedro. So when and where can we meet?' There were few other leads I could pursue at this point. As for Banco Imperio, for now I'd heed Pedro's advice and steer clear. For now.

'I will call her to arrange something and let you know.

Now, if you wait here I will return shortly with the keys to the apartment. I see you've brought your bag.'

The dilapidated old building was down a little lane near the Miradouro de Santo Estevao. The apartment itself was up three flights of stairs. It boasted one bedroom, a bathroom that needed re-plumbing and, as its only redeeming feature, a living room with a small balcony that looked down towards the port; and in the corner of the room, a landline telephone. The furniture was sparse. At the back, leading off the kitchen, was an outdoor iron staircase which accessed a courtyard below. Washing hung from poles off the windows of other apartments and even at this time of night the sounds of neighbours chattering over their balconies, the music from local radio stations and children playing, all served to remind me of normal lives being lived by normal people.

Pedro had stopped off at a supermarket and now we filled the fridge with basic provisions, including a few beers.

'Take good care, my friend,' he said as he handed me the keys.

CHAPTER 11

'Can you find your way to Alameda da Universidade?' Pedro asked the next morning. 'There's a café near the university where we can meet Mariana. Noon okay?'

Having spent most of the night worrying about Claire, I'd eventually fallen into a deep sleep at dawn in spite of the sounds of traffic and the neighbours as the city dragged itself awake. Pedro's call had woken me a couple of hours later.

'I'll be there,' I said.

Mariana Da Cunha had walked from her office at the nearby university. As she entered she greeted a group of students who were drinking coffee in a corner of the café with a friendly wave. Pedro had told me she worked as a senior lecturer at the Faculty of Psychology and had her own counselling practice as well. Prior to this she'd been a nurse. She made her way over to where we were sitting and Pedro introduced us.

After we'd exchanged pleasantries she addressed me

directly. 'Pedro tells me you have an interest in Kazunda, Mr McKinnon. Tell me how I can help you. Or perhaps how you can help me?'

She was an attractive woman with wavy, dark brown hair and darkish skin. She took off her jacket and slung it over the back of the chair. She was wearing a tight-fitting black roll-neck sweater and a short burgundy-coloured skirt over black leggings.

'We believe a large shipment of arms is on its way there by sea,' I said. 'All the information we've so far gathered suggests that a political upheaval is imminent, although that's not the reason I'm involved.'

'To overthrow the government? A coup do you mean? That would be a blessing, but not an easy task. Who is planning this?'

'I don't know. I believe a man called Jawad Mendesa may be involved but …'

Mariana threw back her head in a gesture of disgust. '*Bastardo!* If he gains power the situation will not improve, you can be sure of that. They say it was him and his father who,' she hesitated, 'who were responsible for the death of my own father, and my brother too. They are animals – worse than animals. And I believe he has something that is very dear to me. If I ever find it, it will be at the moment of his death, I swear.' Her eyes were narrowed for an instant, cold and hard, revealing her burning hatred for the man.

This was not the compassionate nurse turned psychologist I'd been introduced to.

'I'm sorry. Tell me what is your interest in this matter?'

'I represent the insurers of the ship that is carrying the weapons. We believe the owners may have been deceived into taking on this cargo, or maybe not. That's what I'm trying to find out. If the ship's owners loaded the arms knowing they were intended for use in an illegal military operation, then their insurance cover would be void.'

'I see,' said Mariana looking doubtful. 'And so how can I help you?'

'Pedro here told me a little of your story; also that you had connections with other *retornados* here in Portugal who would like to see the wrongs of the past put right. I'd like to learn more of these ideas, or plans.'

She looked around the café, which was filling up with more noisy students. 'What, for your insurance claim?' She arched an eyebrow to express her doubts as to my flimsy cover story. 'This is not a good place to talk of such things. Come to my apartment where we may discuss it in private.'

'If you're sure,' I said, uncertain of how useful she was going to be. 'I don't wish to impose upon you. I appreciate these are not easy matters.'

'On the contrary, I think of little else. Come, we shall go now.'

'I cannot,' said Pedro. 'I have a survey to attend this

afternoon. Go with Mariana and if you need me you know how to find me.'

***

Mariana lived in a larger and more comfortable version of the apartment Pedro had found for me. It had an unobstructed view down to the Tejo estuary and the sea beyond, and was on a higher floor, removed from the noise of the traffic. She lived there alone, she told me, since her mother had died a few years previously. She made coffee and served it with a plate of *pasteis de nata*. We sat opposite each other.

'Delicious but fattening,' she said.

'Everything delicious is fattening,' I said biting into one of the custard tarts.

'You don't look as if you need worry,' she replied pouring the coffee and helping herself to one. Then she began her story.

'Kazunda is a very beautiful country, Mr McKinnon, but it is also a troubled one. We Portuguese, both our missionaries and our traders colonised it in the fifteenth century. We made contact with the king of the Bakongo tribe and over the years, the Portuguese, Dutch and English established trading posts and logging camps; also small palm oil factories. Trade grew, including the slave trade, and so did the number of European settlers. Things became very competitive and resulted in much conflict amongst them.

'Eventually Portugal claimed sovereignty and Kazunda became a protectorate. For many years there was peace and our little country prospered, especially when oil was found off the coast. But as you know, in 1974 we had our very own coup here in Portugal, the so-called Carnation Revolution. This led to the end of our empire and the colonies were gradually given their independence, just as with your British Empire.

'I was born in that same year, 1974, in the capital, Kazunda City. My father had been born there and his father and grandfather before him. He was a wealthy man. We lived in a fine old colonial house with beautiful gardens and many staff. For the first few years of independence everything was fine, but then tribal rivalries destabilised the country and eventually civil war broke out. My father was determined to stay on. He had no desire to live in Portugal. He was a foreigner here. But things got worse in Kazunda.'

She stood up and gazed out from the balcony and the city to the sea beyond, reliving the past.

'Is it hard for you, looking back like this?' I asked. She turned to face me, her expression softening as she came back into the present, and I saw now what a lovely looking woman she was when her anger melted away, her features radiating inner calm and a natural compassion.

'No, no. It is all right. It is easy to slip back into the past when it brings back so many memories. But in the end my father ordered my mother and me to leave, to return here to Lisbon. He and my brother would stay on and send for us when peace returned. That was the plan. We did not want to go but we had little choice. I remember it so well. On the day of our flight our bags were packed. My mother, Maria, our house maid, and I were taken to the airport by our driver. Saying goodbye to my father and my brother, Nicolau. He was only nineteen, so brave.

'We returned here, to this apartment. Every day we spoke with them by telephone. Then things got worse and there were no communications. Eventually we learned from others who got out what had happened. The soldiers led by the Mendesas – they were savages not soldiers – had come to the house with machetes and butchered them: my father, Nicolau, all our staff.' Her voice was breaking as she spoke. 'Do you know what our house, our home became for a while, until the Mendesas built a mansion for themselves on the coast? It was taken over by the Minister of Security: Jawad Mendesa's father. He was their spymaster, a torturer and an executioner. There was and still is no justice as we know it. Anyone who opposes the state, and the rule of the *bastardo* Eduardo Loma, who calls himself president nowadays, is imprisoned and very often tortured before being executed.

'After independence, Loma's uncle seized all the land and the properties of the Portuguese and handed them to his cronies. Eduardo Loma – his own nephew – murdered him in the 1990s . I know, it's confusing but it is all about nepotism there now, and it is chaos. Such a beautiful land ruined. I've never been back but every day I think of it, of how it was in my childhood.'

She walked over to a small cabinet in the corner of the room. She moved with a natural, languid grace. She selected a vinyl record from a cupboard, placed it on a turntable and the strains of Fado music filled the room.

'Amalia Rodrigues: do you know of her?'

'No. Pedro took me to a restaurant where there was Fado. The music is haunting, sad.'

'You haven't heard of her? I can't believe it,' she chided. 'She is dead now but is still our Queen of Fado.'

The record was lightly scratched, which only added to the melancholy sound of the music.

'Do you like it, Mr McKinnon? It's true, some of it is sad, but not all.'

'Angus, please. Yes, I do. Pedro told me the songs are about women waiting for their menfolk to come back from the sea.'

'Some are, yes. If it is sometimes forlorn then it suits our national psyche. And if some of the songs tell of women waiting for their menfolk to return, then perhaps that is why it is so poignant to me. Because so often they didn't.

'But let me tell you this,' she went on, changing her

tone. 'The men who rule Kazunda have impoverished the land and terrorised its people. They rule with impunity, not through any democratic process or by rule of law, only through a false sense of entitlement, through greed and the craving for power. And I would like nothing better than to see them overthrown. But by Jawad Mendesa? No! He is no better than the rest of them.'

'So what of the future?'

'We *retornados* have not abandoned the land where we were born and grew up. But we feel helpless, and many are old now. I would make a stand. I would return there if I thought I could make a difference. And if you go there then I will accompany you.'

'I'm not sure I'll need to go,' I said. 'And even if I do, from what you say it would be dangerous for you to return there.'

'I know the place and the people. I still have contacts there, old friends. It was my childhood home. You will need a guide. It is not an easy place to move around in. And I can certainly help you get a visa through the embassy here. But if there is to be a coup it will not be safe there. You will need someone who knows the place.'

'Tell me more about the country,' I said altering the course of the conversation. 'I've read its forests and wildlife are under threat: illegal logging, hunting for bush meat ...'

'Yes, the Rio Chitoka Basin, along with the Congo, makes up one of the most important wilderness areas left on earth. Away from the coast the country contains rivers, forests and swamps. It is teeming with life: lowland and mountain gorillas, chimpanzees, forest elephants and over three-hundred other species of mammals; a thousand species of birds; and six hundred species of fish. And there are approximately six thousand species of tropical plants in the Rio Chitoka Basin.

'Kazunda has been inhabited by humans for more than fifty thousand years. There are over a hundred ethnic groups and outside Kazunda City their lives and wellbeing are linked directly and intimately to the forest.

'The people there are among the poorest on earth and yet it produces more oil than anywhere else in Africa, and there are proven diamond deposits in the mountains and possibly off the coast too. But all this means nothing if it cannot be shared amongst the people. So you understand, the struggle must continue: *A luta continua!* we say. The struggle continues. It was the rallying cry of the FRELIMO movement during Mozambique's war for independence, but we have adopted it.'

She had become fervent again, her eyes burning. 'If you go, then promise me you will take me, please!'

'The best I can do is promise to let you know and we can meet again. As you say, I might need help getting a visa.'

'I will return one day, somehow,' she said, speaking more pensively now. 'And if there is to be a coup, then there may be opportunities to restore stability, if not democracy. I may not get another chance. But do not underestimate me, Angus. I am a very determined woman.'

She didn't need to tell me that.

CHAPTER 12

Grant Douglas had ensconced himself in a deluxe suite at the Palacio Hotel in Estoril, twenty minutes down the coast from Lisbon. It was his kind of place, he said.

'Did you know that because this country was neutral during the war half the European royals pitched up here to escape the chaos back in their homelands? They stayed in a kind of enforced upmarket exile. It was known as the Coast of Kings.'

He went on to tell me how, while the Palacio was the favoured home of the royals, it was also the haunt of German and British agents who used to drink in the hotel bar and, it is said, even socialise together. 'Even the chambermaids were on one side or the other,' he continued, 'and sexy suntanned German agents posing as Swiss neutrals would lie out on the beach ready to seduce lonely Allied spooks missing their home comforts. I've been reading all about it. Every night the casino was packed with aristocrats, spies, diamond smugglers … They say even back then it left *Casa-*

blanca, the movie I mean, in the shade. Imagine that will you? *Casablanca* on steroids!'

'Changed days eh, Grant. Just you and me now. Have you been to the hospital?'

'Sure, yesterday. The kid's in a bad way but they say she'll pull through. You saw her, right?'

'Yes. She was still unconscious and on the ventilator. That was two days ago.'

'She was conscious when I went. Asking where you were, of course. I spoke to the doctor too. They're optimistic but it'll take time. She needs a bit of surgery.'

'I'm going to the hospital when we're done here. But I'm worried about her safety in that place. I spoke to Summers and he said he'd arranged something.'

'She's safe there, don't worry. They've got a full security detail on it. Summers has my back too but he said you didn't want a minder. Is that wise?'

'Yes, I saw your guys when I came in. Inconspicuous they were not. I'm watching out for myself thanks, so don't worry about me.'

He laughed. 'I won't. It's your funeral, and you're deniable anyway.'

'Thanks. What about the children? Is Edward there?'

'No. He's in the States on business. The kids are staying in Edinburgh – I've told Phyllis to keep an eye on them. And the nanny's there too, of course. Her mother's coming down to visit her here.'

'Do you think that's enough? For the kids I mean,' I asked. 'Shouldn't we have a proper security team assigned to them?' After what had happened to Zoe only months before I was getting concerned for the welfare of anyone associated with the IMTF, even indirectly.

'You're right. I'll get onto it. But I want to hear your theories as to who did this. First you, then Claire? They could have killed both of you but they didn't. Why?'

'I'd like to know the answer to that too. They're either careless or they have a convincing way of scaring off people they don't get along with.' I told him about my meeting with Mariana and what she'd said about Mendesa.

'I'm guessing that Mendesa got wind of us via his contacts in Credit Sud and Banco Imperio. I gather Claire was on her way back from a meeting with a contact from Banco Imperio when she got hit. And I'd only just learned about Mendesa from Gudrun Sandmeier when they had a go at me. They knew exactly how to find us both. I'm theorising of course, about Mendesa being behind it.' I added. 'We all have enemies: people we've upset in the past. But I want to hear what you know and how you want to play this, Grant. Then we might have a clearer idea of what they're up to, and where we go from here.'

I still wasn't sure what the end game was supposed to be but I knew he had something in mind or I wouldn't be sitting in front of him now.

'Okay, let me tell you how I see it,' he said getting up from the sofa and walking over to close the balcony doors, either because he was cold or he thought the seagulls were listening in.

'We got this guy Mendesa. And I can tell you this: he's a figurehead and no more. It's the goddamn Russkies behind this scenario. They want more of the African pie. They're sick of seeing the Chinese and the West with all the influence, all the contracts whether it's oil offshore or minerals in the mountains. So let me give you a little lesson in geopolitics.'

'I'm all ears,' I said. I'd already had one from Benny Carasso but it doesn't do any harm to cross-reference the intel you gather.

'Okay. Back in the days of the good ol' USSR, the Soviets were handing out money, arms and manpower into left-leaning anticolonial movements like candy. Their presence in Africa was big. Then with the collapse of the Soviet Union it all went south for them: Russia didn't have the resources or the will to really get behind the old Soviet strategy.

'But hey, twenty-odd years on and they're at it again, establishing a big flat foothold across the whole continent. Sure, China's got the march on them but Russia's interests in Africa are plentiful too now. Africa's an opportunity to ease their isolation and lend credibility to their claim to world superpower status. If you want proof, look at the stats. Russia's trade with Africa has already increased ten-fold so far this century.

'Now then,' he said, getting into the subject. This was what Grant was good at. 'Let's look at where they're investing: a four billion dollar deal to build and operate a crude oil refinery in Uganda; another three billion to develop a platinum mine in Zimbabwe. And that's just in the last few months. I've heard they're looking at dredging offshore for sea diamonds too, on the west coast. These are not small-change deals but if you think that's it, then look at the arms they're supplying. They're not scrupulous like us when it comes to equipping these basket-case armies with weapons.'

'That's pretty rich coming from a CIA man, Grant.'

'Who said I'm CIA? But wait. What about Kazunda? You don't see any Russkies drinking in the bars down there. No Russian-built oil refineries, no Russian tanks on display. Why? Because we have leverage. El Presidente, this guy Eduardo Loma, he's in our pocket.'

'He's a ruthless, murdering despot from what I hear. So this is all about oil, right?'

'Dead right it is. The Kazunda Coastal Oil Company, forty-nine percent owned by Sea-En Oil & Gas Inc. of Houston, Texas. They're pumping half a million barrels a day but that's the least of it. Kazundan reserves are estimated at forty billion barrels. That's more than Nigeria's. Kazunda is

Africa's richest nation in terms of energy resources. And the US is taking the oil and paying the Kazundan government fifty-one percent of the proceeds, virtually none of which finds its way into the domestic economy because Loma and his cronies are stuffing their pockets with it.'

'So what's Uncle Sam doing about that?'

'I admit, not a lot. We make protestations in the UN. Loma's promised to hold free elections by the end of the year, which is a few short weeks away. He won't of course, which suits Uncle Sam fine. Sure, you can look like that, but I'm talking realpolitik here. Which brings us right back to the present situation. Mendesa's cut a deal with his pals in the GRU, the Russkies' military intelligence service. And they're the ones who are behind the *Dalmatia Star* charter.'

How did he know all this? It was a reminder that I wasn't the only one investigating the case. Grant had access to intelligence material I'd never get within a mile of.

'And Horvat's the broker, right?'

'Broker, case officer, fixer … He's an old pal of the GRU going back to the Balkan wars in the nineties. And you can probably blame him for Babic's murder as well.'

'He said he'd arrived in Lisbon the same day as me. Can we get that checked?'

'Sure.'

'He could have boarded the ship the previous night, committed the murder then returned to Lisbon.'

'How would he do that? I thought they kept a gangway watch? Anyway, the accommodation ladder would have been up wouldn't it?'

'Yes, but he could have used a rope and grappling hook to climb over the side, if he was skilled. He certainly looked strong enough. More likely he had one or more of the crewmembers help him.' I silently cursed myself for not having taken a copy of the crew list off the ship.

'And you think Horvat is still on the ship?'

'As far as I know. I'll ask Pedro if he can find out. I don't want to go direct to Lopes, the agent. He's the guy who tipped off Banco Imperio I was in town. And they're in on all this, for sure. But going back to the big picture, what you're saying is the CIA wants to thwart Mendesa's Russian-backed coup in order to keep Loma in power and maintain the status quo. Is that how you see it?'

'In realpolitik terms, yes, exactly. You've got the picture.'

'Not quite. You haven't told me how you're going to do it.'

'Need-to-know basis, buddy, need-to-know. But you'll be in on it once we get down there, don't worry.'

'That's not good enough, Grant. I'm not going anywhere until you tell me how this plays out.'

We stared at each other until finally he broke the silence. 'Did I ever tell you about my time in Laos back in the seventies?'

'You've mentioned it in the past. You said you were just a REMF.'

'Okay, maybe I was rear echelon back in Vientiane. I was a young guy. I wanted to do my bit up there at Long Tieng but I was a law student not a seasoned agent or a fly-boy like the Air America guys and the Ravens. I went up there a few times. What a place. They said it was the busiest airport in the world measured by daily take-offs and landings.'

'Yes, and Laos was and still is the most heavily bombed country in the world – ever.'

'That may be so, but the purpose of the CIA being in Laos was exactly the same as why we need to be in Kazunda now. We were fighting the tide of Communism then. And now the Russians are at it again. Only it's called Putinism this time. But I don't see a big difference between then and now.'

That was a bit of a stretch but I let it go. I sensed Grant had unfinished business. I had the feeling he regretted not being given a more active role back in Laos and saw Kazunda as an opportunity to redeem himself. I waited for him to continue.

'I've got contacts down there. An Air America pilot who went bamboo back in Laos then pitched up in Angola when we had that little war going with the Soviets. UNITA was our proxy and the Cubans were fighting on behalf of the Sovs. This guy Carlos Cordeiro was a Portuguese American. He'd rejoined the Cousins by this time so was cosying up to the Soviet- and Cuban-backed MPLA – the People's Movement for the Liberation of Angola. He was feeding high-grade intel back to Langley. One of the best doubles we had back then.'

'And now?'

'He's still with us under non-official cover and providing good intelligence on what's going down politically in Kazunda. And he's the guy who found out that a small platoon of mercenaries boarded the *Dalmatia Star* off the coast of Morocco a week ago.'

This was the first I'd heard of mercenaries boarding the ship. 'So what's the plan? You and I go down there with six-guns blazing, right?'

'I told you about Sea-En Oil & Gas. They've got a semi-submersible floatel – a living-quarters platform located bang in the middle of the main oilfield, nine miles off the coast: the *Sea-En Resolution*. Within the past week we've had surveillance and comms equipment fitted specific to this operation, manned by a team of surveillance experts. And we've got a team of Navy SEALS on board too. We're heading down there tomorrow.'

'Then what?'

He turned to face me. 'We put a stop to Mendesa and his gang by all means at our disposal. But understand this: what we don't do is create a direct confrontation between Russia and the United States of America.'

'A proxy war then?'

'Let's just call it an operation.'

'Why do we do this, Grant?'

'Do what?'

'Us, the Cousins, the Russkies. We back maniacs like Loma and Mendesa then when it all goes wrong we spend the next fifty years or more dodging all the crap from the politicians, the media, our own people. Korea, Vietnam, Laos, Chile, Nicaragua, Afghanistan, Iraq … It never seems to work out how it's supposed to.'

'You're being a little naïve aren't you? If you're talking about the CIA, they intervene in good faith to fight the spread of communism, or today, the less than benign influence of the Russians, and give the local folk a better shot at a prosperous future.'

'At the hands of a Loma or Mendesa? Now who's being naïve? If these places are to move on then we need to make a bit more of an effort to identify the right kind of local people and support them: in conflict if necessary, but in building a good peace afterwards.'

'I agree. And the CIA today is not the same outfit as it was back in the seventies and eighties, believe me.'

'I hope you're right, Grant.'

CHAPTER 13

We flew from Lisbon to Casablanca, then on to Pointe-Noire in the Republic of Congo, both with Air Maroc.

'Did you get to see Claire last night?' Grant asked as we sipped champagne.

'Yes.'

'And?'

'She'd just had a four-hour operation. She was barely conscious. She wasn't making much sense.'

In fact she had made some sense. Holding my hand she'd asked me to tell her about the mill conversion on the island. 'I want to hear everything,' she'd said. 'When I'm better take me there and I'll help you furnish it. I'll make it a home.' If you get better, I'd thought.

'Claire'll make it, Gus. Don't worry. Just focus on what we gotta do right now.'

'I'll do that, Grant.' Thinking about the job in hand made it easier not to think about Claire.

From Pointe-Noire the journey became less orthodox.

An unmarked Pilatus Porter STOL aircraft was waiting on the far side of the runway and we were taken from our incoming flight, across the tarmac by a man in overalls who hauled our bags behind him. There was no sign of Immigration or Customs.

Our pilot, a lean, deeply tanned man in his sixties, neatly dressed in a white shirt with epaulettes, introduced himself as Carlos Cordeiro.

'Hey! I wouldn't have recognised you, old buddy,' cried Grant.

After much hugging and back-patting between the two of them Grant and I boarded the little aircraft while Cordeiro walked around it conducting his pre-flight checks. I wondered whether this was done to reassure us of his competence or because he really was a pro. Since he'd survived wars flying around in Laos and Angola I reckoned he knew what he was doing. The transfer had taken less than twenty minutes but in the sweltering heat of equatorial Africa my clothes were sticking to me. Grant was wearing an expensive-looking khaki safari outfit tailored from a lightweight material.

'You alright there, Gus?' he asked as we took our seats. He was keen to include me in all his high-spirited camaraderie. Cordeiro boarded the aircraft and began his pre-flight, start and pre-taxi checks before taxiing down the runway.

'I'm just fine thanks. How long's the flight?'

'About four hours,' Cordeiro answered from the cockpit in front of us. 'Beers in that cool box behind you. Help yourselves.'

We took off with all the noise and drama of a small, single-engine aircraft on a potholed runway and headed out into the Atlantic before turning south towards our destination. I reached for a cold beer and offered it to Grant. He declined saying it was important to keep a clear head. I opened the can and took a long swig, at which point Grant suddenly changed his mind and opened one for himself. Then he moved forward to sit beside Cordeiro in the cockpit while I sat back and tried not to remember a flight in an identical aircraft years before which had nearly ended in disaster when we were buzzed by two hostile MiG fighters over the North Sea.

The runway at Pointe-Noire had been as smooth as silk compared with that of the optimistically named Kazunda International Airport, but Captain Carlos took it in his stride and we touched down just as the equatorial night had fallen from the sky like a damp dark shroud. We bade farewell to Cordeiro with Grant promising him he'd be in touch and again, with no time to look around, we were whisked across the runway, this time by a couple of burly Americans in overalls emblazoned with the logo of Sea-En Oil & Gas, Inc. A small four-seater Robinson helicopter with similar company markings was waiting with its rotor blades turning. This time the pilot was José, a friendly, hefty local Kazundan who'd been trained in the US. Within minutes we were strapped in, luggage aboard, life-jackets to hand and headsets on, airborne again on our way out to the *Sea-En Resolution*, nine miles offshore.

'Smooth journey so far,' Grant remarked as we gained height. 'What do you think of Cordeiro?'

'Seems okay.'

'That's pretty damn non-committal even for you.'

'I don't know him. What were you two talking about? Pick up anything new?'

'Mostly talking about Laos back in the day. It was the largest paramilitary operation ever undertaken by the CIA – over three hundred pilots and eighty-odd aircraft including these Porters.'

'Air America? Weren't they involved in drug-running? Opium for some general's heroin plant in return for him supplying local soldiers from his Hmong tribe?'

'Hah! That was the rumour but I never saw any evidence. You'd need to ask Cordeiro that one.'

Then we were in sight of the oilfield. I counted a dozen rigs all lit up like Christmas trees, spread out across the dark sea ahead of us. And in the centre was one bigger and brighter than the rest.

'There she is, ready and waiting for us.'

'Rather conspicuous isn't it?'

'I told you, Gus, stop worrying for Chrissakes.'

I'd remember those words for a long time to come. We were well out from the shore, still five or six miles south-east of the floatel and in plain sight of it when a bolt of white light suddenly shot across the night sky. As we watched it struck the side of the floatel's superstructure with an explosion of light followed by a muffled boom clearly audible above the racket of the helicopter.

'Jesus Christ!' yelled José.

'Missile!' shouted Grant as flames engulfed the floatel lighting up the sky and the sea around it.

And minutes later: 'It's going over!' And we could see the blazing mass of steel slowly keeling over before our eyes as José spoke.

'Lose height, José, and approach it,' I shouted. 'There may be survivors in the water.'

The helicopter dropped close to the water heading towards the rig. For a few tense minutes none of us spoke as we raced a few feet above the sea's surface. As we came round the far side of the rig José transitioned from forward to hover. We were close enough now to feel the heat from the inferno. The thing was burning white hot, the sea ablaze in patches where pieces of wreckage had been blown from the superstructure by the explosion. The whole area was bright as day. But there was not a soul in the water.

'If you want me to land on the sea we have an emergency float system I can deploy,' José shouted, 'but very dangerous to do.'

'No,' Grant replied. 'Just hover here for now.'

No sooner had he spoken than a second missile struck sending more flames shooting into the sky. A blast of hot air pushed the helicopter violently over to one side.

'Where're they firing from?'

'I don't know, Grant. How long do you want to hang around here for?'

'This is futile,' he said. 'No one'll survive that and I'm not going to compromise the mission any further. We're outta here. José! Head for the coast, but head south first, away from the direction of fire.'

José needed no further encouragement. Gaining some height he transitioned again from hover to forward and, still flying low, headed south-south-east.

Grant didn't need me to tell him that whatever happened now, the mission was already critically compromised. None of us spoke. We knew that whoever had targeted the missiles at the *Sea-En Resolution* might have us in their sights now.

'See the lights ahead?' I said. 'That's the coast south of the city. It can't be far.'

But before he could reply there was a loud whoosh and we were blown forcefully sideways again as a missile shot past. Only now it was aimed at us. José weaved, ducked and dived, hurling the little helicopter around in an attempt to evade what we knew was coming. I was beginning to think we'd escaped when the next missile struck and we were thrown sideways again, only this time it struck its target.

José shouted: 'It's hit the tail rotor.'

As it lost its thrust the helicopter began to spin. There are those who will tell you that an emergency landing can be made in such circumstances, but that's not what happened to us. We just plunged into the sea hitting the water in a cascade of spray and a cacophony of noise as the machine tried to rip itself apart. Any hope that we had sufficient buoyancy to keep us afloat long enough to escape in an orderly fashion was soon dispelled. And as we went down I realised we were turning over too. We were upside down in the water, strapped into our seats, sinking fast – and in complete darkness.

An emergency light came on casting an eerie glow around us. As I unbuckled my seat belt José yelled: 'We must wait until the water equalises inside before we can open the door. There are lifejackets under the seats. Put them on now!'

Water was gushing in fast as we sank into the darkness. I looked at Grant. He turned to me: 'This is it, Gus.'

'Just unbuckle, grab the lifejacket and turn yourself the right way up. We'll be fine,' I yelled. The water was already around our waists. We disconnected the belts and struggled to manoeuvre ourselves upright. Only then could we put our lifejackets on. The water rushed in and rose around us. And as it reached our necks José shouted: 'Get ready to breathe deep and pull yourselves out the door!'

Even with the water in the cabin equalising with the ocean outside, it took an interminable time before he managed to free the door by bracing himself and kicking at it with his feet. He went out first and hung outside ready to haul us out. But Grant was still struggling to get his lifejacket on, a look of panic frozen on his face. I grabbed his arm and leaned across to help him. He suddenly came to and, not bothering to fasten the device, dragged himself to the door. In a state of near panic we both fought our way out of the sinking coffin, our lungs bursting.

We broke the surface, José first, followed by Grant and myself. It had been a miraculous escape. Disorientated, we trod water while assessing our situation and realising our troubles were not over. Behind us was the flaming wreck of the *Sea-En Resolution*. Ahead we could make out the surf as it hit the shoreline, perhaps a mile away; it was difficult to tell in the dark.

'You both okay to swim ashore?' José called out.

'No choice,' Grant replied, still struggling to fasten his lifejacket.

'Take it slow. We must save our strength,' said José as we struck out. 'There is a current. Don't try and fight it, but it will take us further south.'

It was further than I'd imagined. We were in the water for an hour before we even heard the sound of the waves crashing onto the beach. Grant was tiring and I swam behind him giving him what encouragement I could. The water wasn't cold but that was little comfort knowing there were tiger sharks in these seas which would attack without provocation.

But after another half-hour the breakers finally swept us onto the beach and we lay on the coarse sand, panting and coughing up seawater. When I sat up and looked back at the floatel it was still engulfed by fire. A column of black smoke rose up from it and into the night.

'There'll be no survivors from that,' said José.

'Even if there are, there's nothing we can do for them, poor bastards. So much for the citadel,' Grant lamented.

I said: 'There are ten or so rigs close by. They have rescue craft so they'll be searching for survivors.'

I wasn't going to get into a discussion just yet as to how the CIA and the US Navy SEALS with all their combined might and resources could have failed to protect the thing.

We'd come ashore on a narrow strip of black basalt sand. I looked inland to where the beach ended with a low cliff above which was dark and impenetrable jungle.

We trudged along the beach towards a scattering of lights we could make out to the north, all three of us shaken by our escape and from witnessing the horror of the conflagration. Many, perhaps hundreds, would have died, others could still be in the water fighting for their lives, though that seemed unlikely. Grant's plan had gone up in flames along with the floatel. He looked ashen-faced and utterly beaten.

'Where the hell did those missiles come from?' I asked him.

'My best guess is they were fired from a sub. They weren't Mickey Mouse jobs. Certainly the ones that struck the rig weren't. They could have been fired from miles away in the Atlantic. And there's only one actor with the motive and the capability.'

'Are you implying that the Russians have committed an open act of aggression against the US?'

'Yes, that's what I'm implying.'

'I thought the rig was registered in Liberia.'

'Yeah. And that'll allow the politicos to prevent an escalation, for the time being at least, but this thing won't go away any time soon, believe me.'

'If the floatel was attacked by the Russians, someone who knew its real purpose tipped them off.'

'You think that's not what's bugging me too?'

We walked on wrapped up in our own thoughts. It couldn't have turned out worse if we'd planned it. The only positive was that we'd survived – for now.

'How far to the nearest settlement do you reckon?' I asked José.

'Maybe five or ten miles to Kazunda City.'

Our clothes were wet, but worse, our shoes were too – somehow we hadn't lost them in the swim ashore – and it wasn't long before we were all complaining. Our surroundings seemed very alien, at least to Grant and me. To our left was the Atlantic Ocean, its breakers crashing onto the black beach. On our right was the jungle, dark and menacing and filled with the sounds of insects, birds and other unknown creatures.

'God only knows what lives in there,' said Grant as an animal scuffled about, uncomfortably close to the edge of the forest where we walked.

After a mile or so we saw flickering lights. We had reached a river estuary, where a cluster of *pirogue* fishing canoes was beached. This was the Rio Chitoka, Kazunda's main arterial waterway running east then looping northwards for five hundred miles to its headwaters in the mountains.

A man broke away from the group who were squatting by a fire on the sand and lumbered towards us: tall and thick-set. José approached with a wave of greeting and spoke to him. The exchange didn't sound particularly friendly.

He returned and said: 'He won't take us across the river unless he gets paid. I told him we have no money.'

'Here,' I said taking off the cheap digital watch I was wearing, which had withstood submersion after the helicopter had ditched. 'Give him this.'

I handed it to José. Grant had sensibly folded his arms to conceal the Rolex he was wearing. After further discussion José turned back to us.

'He agrees,' he said handing the watch to the fisherman who was now joined by two of his comrades. We followed them to where one of the *pirogues* was lying in the shallows. At their urging we jumped on board and the three men pushed the craft into deeper waters before jumping on themselves, one of them using his paddle to steer with while the other two propelled us forward. The river's flow soon pushed us out towards the sea and the men used all their strength to control the primitive craft, little more than a hollowed-out tree trunk. But they knew the river and in no time we reached calmer waters and could make out the swampy bank clogged with mangrove trees ahead of us.

They headed for a stretch of beach clear of mangrove roots and guided the canoe in. As we clambered out they pointed to a dirt road running along the shoreline before branching off back into the jungle. We parted company and headed towards the distant lights of Kazunda City.

The three of us were tired, wet and dispirited. Now, on this second leg, we'd been walking for what seemed like half the night but would have been no more than an hour when headlights appeared ahead of us coming from the direction of the capital. The vehicle pulled to a stop, its lights holding us in their glare. I could make out a black four-by-four pickup. It had stopped ten yards in front of us. The silhouettes of three men appeared, walking slowly towards us. All three were carrying semi-automatic rifles. They wore black battle fatigues and green berets neatly pulled over to the right and with a silver badge over the eye. I could see now the word *Policia* emblazoned on the sides of the truck.

'*Policia Nacional*,' said José. '*Bastardos!*'

CHAPTER 14

They bundled us into the back of the truck along with two of the cops. The driver slammed the tailboard shut, climbed into the cab and took off in a cloud of dust, swinging round and driving towards the city. The two cops just stared at us belligerently, their rifles across their knees. Had they been tipped off by the fishermen?

'What now?' asked Grant.

'I'll do the talking,' said José. 'If they'll listen,' he added.

We arrived on the outskirts of the town as a grey dawn was breaking. Grant and I had left Lisbon at six the previous morning. We'd been travelling, if that's what you could call it, for twenty-four hours. We were wrecked.

Kazunda City was a dismal place. The town, which Mariana had told me had seen virtually no investment in infrastructure since independence over forty years ago, was a mess of trash-littered, pot-holed streets. Those that weren't paved, and all but the main street were not, were just red dirt tracks. We saw buildings that had been bombed or burned out, victims of various insurrections over the years. Others were pockmarked with bullet holes. Even at this early hour people squatted, staring vacantly from doorways. There was no sign of electricity or running water; and no sense that the place was about to come alive.

We passed the Equatorial, which looked like it had once been the town's top hotel, now a decaying slum with burned-out rooms and no glass in the windows.

As we reached what looked like the town centre we turned off heading east inland for a mile or two before pulling up in front of a solid-looking concrete block. It was the police station.

The cops pushed and prodded us inside, down a long narrow corridor that smelled of sweat, urine and faeces. On our left were cells. We passed four, all crammed full of men, some with their hands clinging to the bars and their heads pressed up close to see who these strangers were. Large eyes peered at us. Thin black arms reached out. There was virtually no noise. It was a bleak, wretched place.

José was taken to a cell at the end of the corridor but Grant and I were guided down another dimly lit corridor to a room where a uniformed officer was lounging with his feet on the desk, smoking a cigarette. He looked like he needed a wash. On the wall behind him hung a photograph in a gilt frame. The man in the picture I recognised as Eduardo Loma, self-appointed and unelected president of the Republic of Kazunda.

'Sit,' said one of the cops who'd brought us in. He shut the door behind him. There were two metal chairs in front of the desk. We sat. The two cops took up positions either side of the door, their rifles cradled in their arms. Then, in what looked like carefully rehearsed posturing, the officer slowly uncrossed his ankles and lowered his feet to the floor. He leaned forward stubbing the cigarette out in an ashtray that was already overflowing. He was short and fat. His grey cropped hair was like a wire brush, his eyes small and black, his nose flat. His jowls hung over the collar of his shirt, which was dark with sweat marks. I was searching for something in his behaviour that could be construed as goodwill. But if it was there, I was missing it.

The cop who had driven us to this place spoke at length to his boss, who sat nodding. Then, with some effort, he stood up and leaned across the desk. The buttons of his black shirt looked like they would burst open at any moment to release his gut.

'*Espião*,' he said slowly, pronouncing the word in three distinct syllables. His voice was high-pitched and he wheezed every time he breathed in. 'You are spies. American spies sent to interfere in our country? We have seen people like you before in our country.' He came round the desk and looked down on us. 'Our president does not take kindly to such interference. In fact, there are several foreign spies in our prison. They have been there for many years. Others though are no longer prisoners. They have been executed, but only after they have told us everything we wanted to know. I have personally interrogated some of these men and let me tell you, they have talked. In fact they have sung like little birds.' He was clearly enjoying his performance but Grant had had enough.

'Listen buddy,' he said, standing up and in the process knocking his chair over behind him. 'We're from an insurance company. We lost our passports with our visa stamps but you can check us out with the Portuguese Consul. We're down here on behalf of the Caledonian Marine Mutual Protection & Indemnity Association to investigate a ship that's carrying a cargo of arms and military vehicles. The ship's been hijacked by a bunch of mercenaries who plan to topple your President Loma there.' He spoke angrily, jabbing his finger at the photo behind the desk. 'They're planning to take over your precious country. It's called a coup d'état and it's coming right at you. The mercenaries on board our client's ship have already blown up a rig belonging to a joint venture between your national oil company and a friendly American partner. Then they attacked our helicopter. It ditched just off the coast a few miles south of here, which explains our presence. And believe me, these guys are headed your way. Sooner rather than later.

'All we're interested in is getting the ship returned to

her rightful owners. You can lock us up here and pull our fingernails out all you like, or you can work with us and turn yourself into a national hero. The choice is yours.'

I was impressed by this masterclass and I could see the officer was listening.

'Your choice,' Grant said again for emphasis and reaching over he took a cigarette from the pack of Marlboros on the officer's desk. 'Got a light?'

It was hard to tell whether the cop believed him or not, but he flicked open his Zippo in one practised movement before lighting Grant's cigarette. I'd never seen Grant smoke: he was a fitness fanatic. But he inhaled without balking and blew smoke right back at the cop. Somehow he'd detected something in the man's body language, some doubt or hesitation that I had missed, and he was exploiting it.

'We shall see,' said the cop, not totally convinced by Grant's story. Then he addressed the guards and left the room leaving them to march us down the corridor to José's cell.

As we walked Grant carried on the charade for the benefit of the cops: 'Gus, we gotta get word back to the owners. Their ship's being used as a weapon to attack this country.'

I turned back to the smarter of the two, who clearly had some English: 'Did you guys see that oil rig go up in flames? And the helicopter go down? You must have, right? That's how you knew where to find us. We appreciate it but you need to let the pilot go. We're all just doing our jobs here, not spying on your country.'

One of them shrugged. 'The boss will decide.'

'Can you bring us drinking water? Something to eat?'

He laughed as we were shoved into the cell with the help of a rifle barrel prodded into our backs, and locked in.

The cell was filthy, the stench from a bucket in the corner overpowering. José seemed glad to see us. I sat down beside him on a crude wooden bench along the wall while Grant paced up and down.

'Did he believe you?' José asked after we'd told him of our encounter with the officer.

'I don't know. It looked like he went off to confer with someone – his superior presumably.'

Grant was getting agitated. 'We could just be left in this shithole to rot, you know.' he said.

And so it seemed. We were in that cell for the whole day and the night and day that followed, with neither water nor food; and no visitors. José struck up conversations with some of our neighbours in the adjoining cells but with little effect. From time to time we'd hear the guards doing their rounds. Occasionally a cell door would open and clang shut as some poor wretch was dragged off, not to face any recognisable form of justice, I was sure.

'We've got to get out of here,' Grant croaked desperately on the sweltering afternoon of the second day. Since early morning we'd been aware of what sounded like a sustained offensive, in the distance at first but getting closer as the day wore on and the thump of heavy ordnance began to shake the building. And as if by divine intervention, moments after Grant had spoken there was a flash of light outside the barred window high on the cell wall, accompanied by a whistling sound and the crash of mortar fire outside. It was followed by another and another until it became a continuous volley. The whole building was shaking under the attack now. Then as we stood frozen, barely able to comprehend what was going on, a shell exploded right outside our cell throwing us to the ground in a cloud of muck and dust. I couldn't hear a thing except for the ringing in my ears. As the dust cleared I cautiously raised my head and looked around. Grant was on the ground on one side of the cell with his hands placed over his head. José lay on the other side looking up. And as we caught each other's attention we were grinning like kids. For between where we were and where Grant lay was a gaping hole in the outer wall of the cell.

Coughing from the dust, we staggered out and onto a patch of bare land where two old police pickups were parked. Other prisoners had found their way out too. One side of the prison block had been blown apart. Three of the prisoners were crowded around one of the pickups trying without success to hotwire it.

Another mortar struck and this time it hit the pickup sending it flying into the air. When it landed men were running from it in all directions. Two lay still and bleeding on the ground.

The mortar fire was coming from the east. It seemed those doing the firing were gaining control of territory on both the seaward and landward sides of the city.

We moved fast across the open land and away from the bombardment.

CHAPTER 15

Our shoes and clothes had dried out, but we were hungry, thirsty to the point of dehydration and exhausted from lack of sleep. The police station was now under sustained attack and the prospect of being recaptured was the least of our worries.

While we were in the cell I'd asked José whether he knew where the Da Cunha family home was. He was pretty sure where to find it and agreed that it might provide a temporary safe haven if we ever got out. He also thought there might still be someone there – old retainers perhaps who had survived the city's upheavals. He didn't know about any other occupants, and whether they might be friendly or otherwise. So now we headed inland towards a range of hills and away from where the mortar fire was coming. The terrain was mostly scrubland interspersed with rough tracks and unmetalled roads. There was little cover, but darkness was falling fast now and the sounds of the assault below faded as we climbed. José led us in a south-easterly direction until we hit a potholed road that wound up the hillside. We followed it, darting off into the undergrowth every time a vehicle appeared. But there was little traffic and after two hours of slogging our way upwards into the cloud forest, we began to see houses: big old colonial bungalows, their timbers rotting away in the inhospitable climate and from the relentless invasion of termites and other wood-eating insects of the forest. Most of these once impressive homes had long since been abandoned. A few looked as if they might still be occupied. All of them were in darkness.

'It's up here somewhere,' said José. We were in a thick, swirling mist now and the air had turned chilly. Back in the days when Portuguese expats sought relief from the heat of the city, this hillside must have offered a welcome retreat. Now it was unloved and forgotten.

We were beginning to doubt whether we were on the right road when we came across an old man sitting on a veranda that looked so rotten it might collapse under his weight. He was watching the city under mortar attack far below as what we now thought could not be the small band of mercenaries alone, but an insurgent force fighting alongside them to battle Loma's forces.

José spoke with him, seeking directions. The old man seemed to know the place we were looking for and we pressed on, cold now, exhausted, but spurred on by the old man's assurances.

Eventually we found it, almost the last residence on the road. The house that had once been Mariana's family home still radiated charm despite its dilapidated state. A winding driveway led steeply up from the road through a riot of flowering trees and bushes. The bungalow itself was large, with a surrounding veranda making it look bigger. Even in the dark I could see the place had been cared for over the years since the family had been so violently torn from it. As we approached a light appeared on the veranda and a woman wearing a loose white dress, carrying an oil-filled lantern and accompanied by a man with an ancient shotgun held in his arms, came down the steps towards us. It was not the first surprise of the day, just the most welcome.

As recognition dawned Mariana Da Cunha cried out: 'Angus! I had no idea whether you were here or where you were. *Meu Deus!* Who are these men with you?'

I introduced Grant and José. 'Welcome to Kazunda,' she said, without missing the irony. 'Come, I cannot say we are safe, but anyway safer than those poor people down below. This is Marco, a dear friend from my childhood days. We played together in this very house. But look at you! Where on earth have you been?' She spoke rapidly to Marco and then to José in Portuguese. 'We can get you cleaned up and fed at least. After that, God only knows!'

As we climbed the rickety steps and followed her across the veranda into the house, Grant asked in a low voice, 'Is she for real?'

'What do you mean?'

'You never said she was a goddess. And here she is in this hell-hole? Jesus!'

Mariana, even under these difficult conditions, was a commanding presence. Within minutes we were sitting in rattan chairs, their cushions faded and musty, clustered around a wood-burning stove with large glasses of water and *Aguardente de Medronhos*, the fruit brandy I'd last tasted with Pedro in the Alfama Fado restaurant, what seemed like a century ago.

'We can offer you only cold showers I'm afraid. We have no electricity and the water would take all night to heat on the stove. You all smell terribly, so Marco here will show you the bathroom and find you some almost fresh clothes. We have food and wine. And then we talk while we eat. How does that sound?'

'That sounds absolutely fine, Ma'am,' said Grant suddenly discovering his smooth-talking and charming, old-style manner. 'You are a gracious host and we thank you sincerely. But this doesn't seem like a secure kind of place for a woman to be.'

'Mr Douglas, there are many good people in this country who only ask to live their lives in peace. If I can do anything to help them, I will. That is why I am here.'

***

I stood under the cold shower for a long time trampling my filthy clothing under foot and wondering once more where this ill-fated enterprise was leading us.

Marco had laid out a faded, loose-fitting old *dashiki* shirt and baggy trousers on the bed for me. I dressed and went back through to the main room, passing by the kitchen from where the smell of cooking came. The cook, another old retainer who had resurfaced upon Mariana's recent arrival, served us food in the dining room where the five of us now sat, an incongruous gathering that circumstances had drawn together in this strange setting.

We were served cassava leaf stew with pieces of emaciated chicken washed down with warm Nocal beer. 'I can't remember having a better meal,' said Grant, echoing my own thoughts.

José decided to take off in search of his parents, who lived on the coast and whose safety he was worried about. We thanked him warmly. Adversity and danger of the kind we'd faced had brought the three of us together in a bond of camaraderie. We told him to keep in touch if possible and wished him well. Then, further fortified by the brandy, the rest of us returned to the living room and, seated round the stove, talked late into the night.

Mariana had only arrived from Lisbon two days earlier having decided not to wait any longer. Although the situation in the country was volatile and news sketchy, she had her sources, mainly via Marco, and had discovered that Jawad Mendesa's mercenaries, as that is who they were she was assured, had established a beachhead north of the city from where they were launching mortar attacks with the aim of dislodging Loma and taking the capital. She'd been told that it was there at the beachhead that a ship had been seen discharging vehicles and men. The convoy had then driven inland to form a north-eastern flank. It would have been from there that the attack on the police headquarters, which had given us our freedom, had been launched. And as we'd surmised, they had been joined by militias loyal to Mendesa.

But to take the capital meant capturing the real prize, Recife Preto or Black Reef, the old Portuguese fort built back in the seventeenth century and so named because of its location on a jagged outcrop of volcanic rock offshore and connected to the mainland by a narrow causeway. Nowadays, Black Reef was the stronghold of Eduardo Loma, the command centre of his regime as well as his presidential palace. On the landward side of the causeway his presidential guard were stationed in a redoubt, a stronghold again dating back to the earliest colonial times and intended to repel any attack before it reached the fort itself.

On the seaward side, the jagged reef provided an effective defence in itself as it stretched for half a mile westwards out into the Atlantic barely submerged under water, making any seaborne assault from that direction risky if not impossible.

Based on what Mariana had learned we speculated that the *Dalmatia Star,* having discharged her lethal cargo and disembarked the mercenaries, might be performing a logistical support role in preparation for the final offensive against Black Reef. It seemed likely that she had also been fitted with weaponry of her own and might be moved further south to provide cover for the land-based mercenary force as they mounted their raid on the fort.

I had thought that the loss of the *Sea-En Resolution* along with all the sophisticated equipment and manpower on board, which collectively would have made the task of warding off Mendesa's assault relatively straightforward, would have devastated Grant; that and what followed with the harrowing experience of being ditched into the Atlantic, maltreatment at the hands of the Kazundan police and the exhausting trek out of the city. The CIA's black op to prop up Loma's corrupt regime had failed spectacularly, and no doubt with momentous geopolitical ramifications to follow. Mendesa was simply a proxy for the Russians, who were out to gain a further boot-print on the continent. From everything we were learning it looked likely Loma's grip on power was weakening by the hour. And that didn't look good for US strategic interests, for Big Oil's Kazundan offshore energy resources, for the CIA or, not least, for Grant Douglas's career prospects.

But Grant was a wily old pragmatist and I could see that his Plan A was rapidly morphing into Plan B as we talked through and attempted to analyse these unfolding scenarios.

'Listen,' he said, draining his brandy glass, 'I'm not going to lose control of this operation. I don't give a rat's ass for Loma and his cronies. And I don't give a rat's ass for what Langley might think of this whole debacle. We can only do what we can now, given the current situation on the ground here.' He didn't tell us whether he felt the IMTF or MI6 would give a rat's ass either.

'Mariana,' he continued, 'you said the good folk of this country wanted peace and stability. Why don't you tell us your version of how that might be realised?'

Whether Mariana approved of what she was hearing or not, she did not say. She just sighed as if she'd heard the question a thousand times. 'I warn you, it is complicated,' she began. 'You know that Africa, perhaps more than anywhere, is a continent of tribes – over three thousand of them. Some tribes get along with other tribes and some don't. Some live alongside other tribes as sociable neighbours, some don't. They fight for power and control instead.

'Here in Kazunda we have many tribes, but mostly they are of Bantu origin. The Ambundu, Ovimbundu, the Bakongo – these are some of the Bantu tribes indigenous to the country. But then we have Benga people, and some others who have emigrated here over time from other regions.

'In Kazunda, the Ambundu tribe is the largest – perhaps thirty-five percent of the population. They speak Kimbundu, and those who have been educated also speak the official language, which is still Portuguese.

'These tribes are further split into clans and it is important to understand the distinction. Clan loyalties are very strong because clan members all know of their extended family ties; so one is loyal to family first, then by extension to the clan. But marriages are normally external of course. I mean outside of your own clan.'

'To avoid inbreeding?'

'Exactly. So in Kazunda, President Loma is of the Ambundu tribe, which I suppose is why people have put up with him for so long, because he can get away with it.'

'And Mendesa?'

'Ah, Mendesa. He claims to be Ambundu too although he is part Portuguese on his mother's side.'

'So how would you restructure the country's political hierarchy?' Grant asked.

'Me?' she laughed. 'You know, just because one tribe is more representative than the others doesn't mean they have the right to govern. There are several fine tribal chiefs who are just and democratically minded, both here in the capital and in other parts of the country. But there is no democratic structure, no system for them to stand in local elections or for parliament. The parliament is a puppet show for Loma to do with as he pleases.'

'And now it's all coming apart as we sit here talking about it,' Grant added.

Mariana was silent for a moment then got up from her chair and stood looking out across the veranda into the mist and the black forest that lay just beyond the garden. 'There is a clan, a people who are part of the Ambundu tribe. This is an unusual situation but the clan's chief is a woman. She is known as a princess due to her standing within the Ambundu. She has done much good in her clan's district. They have formed a local assembly. They work with the elders, with women as well as men. It is like a democracy there. They build good relations with neighbouring clans – even with other tribes. She honours tradition but wants the people to move forward too. I know of her through the foundation I work with in Lisbon. We send medical aid and educational tools, text books and that kind of thing, to the villages. Her name is Nzinga and her assembly is a recipient of our aid packages.

'They say she is descended from Anna Nzinga, the warrior queen who led resistance against the Portuguese then negotiated a peace treaty with us. That was in the sixteenth century. She was from Angola across the border. Queen Nzinga is remembered for her political and diplomatic acumen, as well as her astute military tactics. She has long been thought of as a symbol of the fight against oppression, and so is today's Nzinga. And they say she has inherited her ancestor's fine judgement, and her charisma.'

'You think she'd really make a viable alternative to Loma?' I asked her.

'I don't know. I only know that she is highly regarded by those Kazundans who want peace and order for their country.'

'So where is this little Utopia?' Grant asked.

'It is up the river, the Rio Chitoka. A long way up.'

'Communications?'

'All communications are down now. Radio, TV, the cellular network too,' said Marco.

'How do we get up there?' Grant asked, suddenly impatient. 'I want to see this woman. We've got to make something happen. I can call in military support against Loma or Mendesa but there's no point in doing that unless we have a viable frontrunner to take their place. Otherwise this country of yours will just descend into further chaos and anarchy.'

Grant looked at me. 'What do you make of all this, Gus?'

'You're right. We must talk to someone who commands respect and authority in this place. I trust Mariana's judgement of Nzinga. And it's not like we have an alternative.'

'Okay, so we need to get up there. When can we leave?'

CHAPTER 16

I woke under a mosquito net, bathed in sweat, my mouth dry. But I'd slept for ten hours and after a cold shower and three cups of Côte d'Ivoire coffee I was ready for whatever lay ahead I told myself.

It was raining with all the deafening ferocity of an equatorial storm. Fork and sheet lightning flashed across the sky accompanied by apocalyptic thunder-rolls. Water overflowed the guttering and splashed onto the veranda where we stood watching the drama.

Grant was determined we should meet with Nzinga as soon as possible. That was until Marco greeted us with the news that the only road to Kintani, the township where she held court, was closed.

'Any idea why?' Grant asked.

It was Mariana who replied. 'They say Mendesa's men are sealing off all routes into the city to stop people from the provinces getting in.'

'What about the river?' I asked. 'Is it navigable?'

'There are rapids east of the city but beyond that it's navigable and boats can get all the way up to Kintani. It's not used much these days but with the road closed it's a possibility I suppose. We would need a boat of course,' she said looking at Marco. I could see from their body language that they were on easy terms which each other, born of their past friendship and a mutual trust.

Marco headed off on a little motorbike to make enquiries and returned after a couple of hours to tell us what he'd arranged. The rain had eased off and we sat out on the veranda where it was cooler and formulated a plan so fraught with risk that Grant insisted Mariana stay behind. She just smiled.

We left at dusk that evening. Marco was driving a decrepit UN Land Rover he assured us he'd only borrowed, with Mariana alongside him and Grant and myself in the back. Marco knew another route away from the main road that would take us past the rapids to a small settlement from where we might find transport upriver. His best guess was that the journey to Kintani would take three or four days, that was if all went well.

We rolled, bounced and slithered our way along a track of red mud heading east with the aim of intersecting with the Rio Chitoka some eighty miles or so from Kazunda City. This would place us at the river port a few miles upriver from the rapids, and it was here we hoped to find the ride on up to Kintani.

Again the rain was incessant, the road a quagmire. Either side of us was dark jungle. Marco was twisting and turning the wheel to keep from getting stuck in the deep ruts left by other vehicles. But on three occasions during the five-hour drive, Grant and I had to get out and lay mats in front of each wheel to provide traction.

We saw little traffic in either direction, which was welcome as with the main road closed Marco had feared our track would be crowded with people from the villages trying to reach the capital. More likely they were staying well away for there were reports of attacks by supporters of Mendesa wherever they met resistance from local tribespeople.

Eventually around midnight we turned off onto a narrow track even more treacherous than the one we'd been on. 'Not long now,' Marco assured us.

By the time we reached the river we were weary, hungry and wet.

'I'd never adjust to conditions like this,' Grant said, tactfully conveying what he thought of the place.

The river port was little more than a jetty at the end of the track, which itself went no further. Half a dozen ramshackle wooden huts were scattered along the bank. The jetty, or what was left of it, had partially collapsed into the river as its wooden pilings had rotted away. There was no sign of anything resembling a ferry, only a few *pirogues* beached on the muddy bank.

'We must wait here,' said Mariana. We didn't have anywhere else to go. 'Marco will ask the locals if they know where we can find a boat ride.'

We waited while Marco went down to the river where a group of fishermen were looking at us strangers with mild curiosity. When he returned he was shaking his head. He spoke rapidly to Mariana, who then turned to us. 'The boat left this morning. They don't know when it will return. Usually, they say, within a day or so.'

'Is there any way we can get a message to Nzinga?' I asked.

'Jungle drums?' suggested Grant.

'No. We must wait for the boat,' said Marco decisively.

So we waited. I was glad to have Marco with us. He was a resourceful, optimistic guy, the same age as Mariana – in his forties – hefty, with a big round face that was more often than not covered in a broad smile. He negotiated the use of one of the tin shacks which was dry inside, though there was little else that could be said in its favour. And he bought some fish from the men down by the river. It was three in the morning by the time we finally ate. Marco barbequed the sweet-tasting fish which he'd prepared with the ubiquitous cassava leaf stew washed down with what we hoped was fresh spring water and glasses of *mampoer*, local firewater distilled from the maroela fruit.

Little happened the next day. We waited with growing impatience for the boat to appear from upriver. But only the *pirogues* plied the quiet waters. The highlight of the day was when one of the fishermen hooked a goliath tiger fish. Marco told us the locals believed that if the evil spirit entered one of these things it would attack humans. This particular sharp-toothed predatory monster was almost five feet long.

We talked with some of the villagers, who were eager for news of what was happening in the capital. They shared their food with us and in the evening we joined some of the menfolk and drank *mampoer* round a fire they'd lit on the riverbank.

The following day started the same. I went out at first light when the colours of the forest were vibrant shades of green and a mist hung over the river. The sounds of the birds, monkeys and other creatures, echoed as their chattering, squawking and cooing rang out from the dark jungle. For an hour or so it was cool and refreshing, but well before midday the sun was overhead, as strong as I'd ever known it, the heat and humidity at their most suffocating. As I squelched my way through the undergrowth it wasn't the vividly coloured yet menacing flowers or the hanging creepers that tried to wind themselves around me that I knew I would remember, but the stench of rotting vegetation. The forest was thick with it for no direct sunlight reached here. It was above in the canopy that the wildlife dwelt. I returned to the riverside to join the others. Now, in the flat light of midday, colours were washed out and the river lay viscous and still.

By early afternoon we had all descended into a state of torpor. And I was becoming uneasy as to our reasons for being here. It was a huge gamble to expect that a tribal princess was going to rally to the idealistic notion of democracy and lead this unfledged little nation away from another era of poverty and corruption at the hands of yet one more despot. I didn't want to sound too pessimistic now that we were committed, but I prepared to voice my concerns to Grant and Mariana, if only to initiate a discussion. At that point however, one of the fishermen came running up the path to our hut shouting and pointing up the river.

'It's the boat,' yelled Marco and we made our way down to the bank to see a dark grey motor launch appear in the distance, dwarfed by the jungle around it. As it grew closer I could see three crewmembers – two in the cockpit and another sitting in a recess in the bow manning a machine gun. All three were locals dressed in military fatigues.

As it drew up alongside the jetty ropes were slung ashore and a couple of fishermen tied the craft to the decaying wooden bollards. Marco walked down to meet the crew, engaging the skipper in conversation as he stepped ashore. There was much pointing in our direction.

'Let's join them,' said Mariana and we walked down

to the river bank where Marco introduced us. The skipper spoke Portuguese and Mariana translated.

'I'm telling them what's happening at the coast. They have no signal for their phones but some news has reached them by word of mouth. They've agreed to take us upriver to meet with Nzinga.'

'When can we leave?' Grant asked.

'They will refuel here. And they have some deliveries to make here in the village. We should be ready in half an hour or so.'

'How long will the journey take?' Grant asked.

'Twenty four hours if there are no delays, maybe a little more. It's nearly two hundred miles to Kintani.'

Having refuelled and taken on stores it was four in the afternoon when we finally got underway. Marco had paid one of the fishermen to keep an eye on the Land Rover for us, promising him the same amount on our return if it hadn't been stolen or damaged.

The boat was an old US Navy Patrol Craft or PCF, also known as a Swift Boat. 'This looks like a Mark III. Nice boat when they're well maintained,' said Grant, who was familiar with it from his days in Vietnam and Laos. As we got underway he began to recite its specifications: 'All aluminum hull, fifty foot long, and a shallow draft for patrolling up the coast. Later we used them for work on the rivers – particularly the Mekong of course. They were part of our brown-water navy. Two General Motors diesels, four-eighty horsepower each, and with a range of three hundred plus nautical miles at twenty-one knots, or double that at half speed: ten knots or so, which is what we're doing now I reckon, just about.'

'Were they heavily armed?'

'Sure, ours were: two .50 calibre Browning machine guns in a turret above the pilot house and an eighty-one millimetre mortar combination mounted on the rear deck; plus we fitted an M60 machine gun in the peak tank in front of the forward superstructure; just like this baby's got, see?' He was pointing out its attributes as he spoke. 'These things were used to intercept the Vietcong, but they also moved our own Vietnamese forces around and inserted SEAL teams for counter-insurgency work. Let's get on board and I'll show you round.'

CHAPTER 17

We made good progress that afternoon. Although heading upstream the river seemed still, the current barely moving the sluggish brown waters. As evening fell we pulled into a dilapidated jetty similar to the one we'd left earlier. We clambered ashore and were guided to a collection of huts. Money changed hands and food was produced. Again, cassava stew and this time, bottles of warm beer. The villagers wanted to know who we were and what was happening in the capital. Marco updated them. Where were we going, they asked: to see Nzinga? Yes, to see Nzinga, he said. There was a buzz of conversation. They wanted to know why. There was no doubting that they held her in high esteem. After an hour we prised ourselves away and headed back upriver.

There was neither moon nor stars that night. The cloud cover and the looming jungle rendered the night black but for the boat's searchlight, which scanned the waters ahead looking for mud banks and other obstructions. We moved more slowly now and the jungle closed in on us as the river gradually narrowed. It was an eerie sensation and yet there was a sense of oneness with the natural, unspoilt world around us, undisturbed by man.

' "Going up that river was like travelling back to the earliest beginnings of the world." '

'You quoting something at me?'

'Conrad – Heat of Darkness.'

'Must read that sometime. You know they based the 'Nam movie Apocalypse Now on Kurtz, right?'

I was sitting with Grant on the after deck. He'd been reminiscing about his days in Laos and Vietnam. Although he'd been rear echelon, he'd been out on plenty of exercises on boats like this one. I asked him to tell me more about Cordeiro.

'Carlos? Portuguese, some Chinese blood too. Born in Macau. As you know, ex-Air America pilot in 'Nam and Laos. Air America was one of the CIA's proprietaries. Back in those days they ran a lot of those shady outfits. Carlos was an ace pilot and he went on to join the Ravens. They were mostly former fighter pilots used for forward air control - providing direction for the air strikes against communist Pathet Lao targets. They were supporting the Hmong guerrilla fighters up there.

'When that whole show was winding down Carlos moved to Africa. He fitted in nicely, being Portuguese and familiar with the language and to some extent, the culture.

He was a bush pilot ferrying personnel, arms, all sorts, in and out of Angola, mostly from South Africa and Zimbabwe - Rhodesia in those days. The Angolan civil war had already broken out so it was only natural for the CIA to look him up. They ran a covert invasion of Angola back in the mid-seventies. Used Portuguese private military contractors and Cordeiro was one of them. He helped train the troops who went in to support UNITA, Savimbi's movement. Like I said before, we continued to back them throughout the civil war against the MPLA, who were under the Cubans, and who in turn were proxies for the Soviets of course.'

Mariana had joined us but Grant carried on talking. He didn't seem worried sharing his knowledge of such matters with her.

'By the late eighties Cordeiro was running his own private army made up of some tribe. Then he pitches up here and he's still providing us with good intel on what's going on.'

'Yes!' Mariana interjected. 'The Ambundu tribe. That's how he came to be in Kazunda.'

Grant looked surprised. 'So you know about Cordeiro?'

'Everyone here does. He's close to Nzinga. And she is of the Ambundu people. I told you.'

'I didn't know that about Cordeiro though,' said Grant, clearly shocked.

'And did you also not know that Nzinga is a Marxist?'

'What?' Grant was having trouble processing this. His understanding had been that Cordeiro, as a CIA asset, was fighting the good fight in support of Loma and therefore US interests, thus preserving the status quo. Even if Loma were overthrown and the CIA's plan to prevent Mendesa taking his place failed, if Nzinga had a Marxist agenda and Cordeiro was close to her, wouldn't that place them too close to Mendesa and his Russian backers for comfort? Or if that was too far-fetched, then what about the Chinese? They were way ahead of either the Russians or the Americans in terms of economic and commercial investment and influence in this part of the world. A Marxist government in Kazunda might suit them nicely.

'We need to get a handle on this,' he said, more to himself than anyone. He could see what was already a debacle turning into a full-blown disaster, with him at the heart of it.

'I don't see why this should be such a problem,' said Mariana sharply. 'Don't we want stability and peace here for the people of Kazunda? Isn't that more important than all your political games?'

'Sure, sure. You're right.' He patted her knee affectionately - condescendingly I thought. We all wanted peace and stability for Kazunda, but what was worrying Grant was how he was going to explain to his masters in Langley why he'd allowed power to be handed over to a Marxist tribal princess and her rogue-CIA boyfriend who, if he'd taken up the Marxist ideology himself which seemed possible, was somewhat at odds with the US way of thinking.

'Look,' I said. 'If Cordeiro is backing Nzinga he's maybe just being pragmatic. He's seeing Nzinga as the least worst option if and when Loma's gone.'

'You think?' said Grant. 'Anyway, that's not what's worrying me.'

'What then?'

'When we were flying down from Pointe-Noire I told Cordeiro about our operation.'

'You're kdding! You mean about the *Sea-En Resolution* being your command and control centre from which you planned to defeat Mendesa's forces?' It was my turn to be shocked.

'Yes! For Chrissakes, I thought the guy was one of ours. Suppose he tipped off Mendesa about the rig's real purpose?'

'Would he have had time between you telling him and the attack being launched?'

'That flight from Pointe-Noire down here was four hours. I was only with him for the first half hour. After that he'd have had time to radio a message out. I'm convinced that at least those first two missiles that hit the rig came from a sub. You couldn't destroy a whole structure that size using the kind of lightweight rockets that hit our chopper. And if Cordeiro did tip them off, that makes him a turncoat as well as an accessory to mass murder. He's one clever sonofabitch though: remove the two principal players from the scene and enter stage left his Commie princess.'

'Whatever your cynical plans, Nzinga is the only one who can save the people and reunite the tribes,' Mariana said. 'But she isn't going to fight any CIA proxy war for you. So maybe you're right. She needs Cordeiro to remove both those despots, in which case he is clever. But I hope not too clever for his own good.' She turned to Grant and placed a hand on his arm. 'I think it is time for you to decide what is right by your own conscience. Perhaps it is overdue.'

And with that she got up and walked forward to the wheelhouse.

'What do you think?' Grant asked.

'Forget about Cordeiro for a moment. Like I said, Nzinga is the least worst option. No one can say whether a Marxist regime in her hands can work or not, but if Loma and Mendesa are fighting it out in mutually assured destruction combat, you've got a power vacuum and chaos to follow if there's no one there to fill it. And remember what you said before we left the city. You were all for meeting Nzinga.'

'I guess you're both right. You know, I've only ever met one person like Mariana, Gus, and that was my wife. She died, in a car accident back in the States. Long time ago. I told you about that once didn't I? But she had that inner strength, that self-belief. She was always sure of her opinions and what had to be done. And she stuck to them. There was no ambivalence about her and neither is there with Mariana. I respect that.'

He didn't talk much after that. The night seemed endless. I went forward and talked with Marco about what lay ahead. 'I believe Nzinga is a good person,' he said, 'and she has the support of her clan and her tribe. Whether she can save our country is another matter. It's a gamble. She doesn't know what is happening in the capital. First we must convince her, then she must convince her tribespeople, not just in her region but throughout the country. And then what? She has no army of her own.'

'What if the army switched their loyalty to her?'

'It is possible; also the *Policia*. Both are known to be unhappy with the way the country has been run. But how can she communicate her message to the people?'

'The traditional way in a coup situation is to seize control of the national radio and TV stations,' I said. 'But I agree, there needs to be a rallying cry before then.'

'Word travels fast here even without TV and radio, and without jungle drums. See how the villagers downriver asked what was happening in the capital, where we were going, why were we here? All this will be passed around the whole region. So perhaps you are right. She will need a rallying cry if she believes she is really destined for this role.'

I dozed off after that and when I woke another grey dawn was breaking. Marco handed me a mug of coffee the crew had boiled up. Again, there was a thick mist lying on the river's surface which cleared as the day heated up. I walked back to the afterdeck where I'd left Grant. He and Mariana were propped up against each other.

'They seem to be getting on well together,' said Marco. 'I'll get more coffee.'

I thought of Claire back in Lisbon. I was missing her badly. What would she make of this place and of what we were doing here? The sounds of the jungle coming alive could be heard above the noise of the boat's engines. Monkeys screeched, birds whooped and insects buzzed. Occasionally a fish would jump, stirring the still waters. The four of us sat there, watching and listening.

'I wouldn't want to fight a war in this jungle,' said Grant. 'In 'Nam and Laos we just defoliated to locate the enemy.' No one passed comment on that.

Marco went forward to the cockpit. On his return he announced: 'We'll reach Kintani in another couple of hours they say.'

No sooner had he spoken than the sound of the boat's engines was drowned out by another noise from behind us. Alerted, the skipper instinctively turned the boat in towards the bank and the shelter of the jungle's canopy. We turned to see two helicopters appear round a bend in the river, one behind and off to the left of the other.

'Holy shit!' shouted Grant. 'They're Havocs – Russian

military choppers. What the hell are they doing here?'

'Get below!' I yelled. It was impossible to say whether the Havocs had spotted us or not, but I guessed that even if they had we were not their prime target. One of our crew was manning the forward machine gun, tilting it up towards the choppers as they skimmed low over our heads. But there was no exchange of fire. The Havocs just kept on their course, sweeping over us and on up the river.

'They're heading for Kintani,' said Mariana, voicing what everyone feared.

CHAPTER 18

A furious argument erupted between the skipper and his crew, with Mariana and Marco joining in. I didn't need to understand the language to tell what it was about: whether we should continue upriver to join what could be a very one-sided confrontation, or turn round and seek safety downstream.

Mariana talked rapidly to the skipper in Portuguese who was shaking his head. Then she turned to us: 'We must go on, at least get close to see what's happening and whether we can help. I'm not saying we head straight into a battlefield, but we need to know.'

There was no argument from Grant or myself. I spoke directly to the skipper, who I knew had some English. 'What happens here at Kintani now will have a bearing on the future of your country,' I told him, 'for you and your people, your family. We may be able to influence the outcome. The reason we're going there is to persuade Nzinga to help us overcome Mendesa and his mercenaries; to bring peace and democracy to Kazunda. Is that not what you want?' I figured Mariana must have said pretty much the same to them but there was no harm in pushing the point home.

We prevailed. The crew were clearly terrified at the prospect of running headlong into an airborne assault but the skipper had had his mind made up for him and, as dusk fell, we edged out following a course closer to the bank and the cover of the trees. The lethargy that had settled over us was gone now. There was enough adrenalin between us to propel the launch itself upriver.

'Thank you,' said Mariana. 'I wasn't winning the argument. I think you swayed it.'

In no time it was dark. We were getting closer and as we rounded a bend we could hear the sound of gunfire. Grant spoke to Mariana: 'Ask the skipper what kind of firepower they've got up there in Kintani will you? The locals I mean.' But the skipper addressed us directly.

'Mortars I know, and assault rifles.'

'Mortars? What kind of rounds do they fire?'

'I don't know.'

'Mortars are pretty useless against aircraft,' said Grant, 'unless you get very lucky. Same with AKs.'

I turned to Grant. 'Any idea what weaponry those choppers were carrying?'

'Normally they'd be equipped with 30mm Shipunov autocannon, rockets too, but I saw no sign of the missile racks on either of them. No, I reckon they're just firing M16A2s. You can tell from the three-round bursts we heard. It's what distinguishes them from AK47s. God knows where they got hold of them.'

Once again Grant had surprised me with his knowledge of the weapons of war. I thought of him in the office back in Leith with his red bow tie and matching braces over a blue shirt; and of the highly cherished fleet of old Bentleys he kept down at his converted Reiver tower house in the Scottish Borders. But if Grant's cover was that of a sedentary maritime lawyer, it didn't show now. He was over sixty but had always kept himself in good shape. Now there was a glint in his eye I'd not noticed before. Was it the smell of battle that was stiffening the sinews and summoning the blood I wondered?

Suddenly one of the Havocs reappeared round a bend heading downstream and straight at us, its searchlight scanning the river and the bank. And without warning our forward gunner began firing off a continuous volley of rounds.

'Christ! He'll give away our position,' yelled Grant above the noise. At first the helicopter continued on its course. Then, as we watched, it rolled in a tight circle, turned, then tilted forward to attack. And as its searchlight fixed its beam on us I waited for the strafing to follow. But before he could line us up, the impossible happened. Our gunner, swivelling his machine gun round, sprayed the chopper's exposed cockpit with gunfire, got lucky and must have hit the pilot or some critical part of the machine for the aircraft began a steep climb, its engine noise reaching a crescendo as it headed away from the river and up over the forest canopy. Transfixed, we watched as it reached an almost vertical trajectory before falling back and crashing through the trees, its rotor blades thrashing the branches as it came down, and on impact exploded in flames.

'Jesus! One down… Do you reckon they're Mendesa's, those helos?' Grant shouted to Marco.

'Those helicopters are the national army's. They bought them from the Kenyans two years ago. But who knows who is flying them now.'

'And why attack Kintani?' I said. 'If it is Loma, surely he has enough trouble to deal with in the capital without courting trouble up here.'

'It could be that Mendesa's mercenaries have seized them,' Marco replied. 'Nzinga is a threat to both Loma and Mendesa, whoever takes power. And she commands the whole district around here, not just Kintani, so I guess whoever sent the helicopters wants to pre-empt any resistance.'

We moved forward slowly until we reached a landing – another broken-down wooden jetty, like the others on the river. We could see the remaining Havoc now like some giant raptor circling around the village centre no more than a quarter of a mile away, the sound of its gunfire audible above the clatter of its engine. Then it dipped down below the trees.

'Is it landing?'

'Don't know.'

Ever practical, Mariana was already busy assembling her improvised paramedic kit and now we rushed to disembark from the launch.

'It's a slaughterhouse,' said Grant gesturing up the path towards the settlement. 'It would be madness to walk into that while the battle's still raging. We must wait.'

'But we may be able to help,' Mariana replied, desperation in her voice.

Grant cut her short. 'We can only help if we're alive. You must see the sense in that.' She just stared at him in frustration, but she knew he was right.

We didn't have long to wait. Within minutes the Havoc rose into the air again and headed back downriver. But as the sound of its engine faded it was replaced by something worse: the moaning and wailing of the injured and the dying. We headed up the path and arrived at the edge of the central square to confront a scene of carnage.

The flickering light cast by oil lamps and torches revealed a sight that would haunt my dreams, twisting them into grotesque nightmares. The injured cried out, some crawled, others knelt over their kin, and many lay where they had fallen. Blood spread across the earth in dark patches. In that dancing light the massacre became a scene more dreadful than anything I had ever witnessed. Looking around I estimated there were eighty to a hundred people lying there, dead or wounded.

Straightaway Mariana began a methodical triage process of tagging the dead, those injured beyond help and those who would benefit the most from treatment. Grant was anxious to find Nzinga and took the launch skipper with him to look for her. The remaining two crewmembers roamed around the clearing in anguish, looking for family, neighbours, loved ones. On Mariana's instruction, Marco went off to search for any local medical facilities and supplies he could find. I remained to help her as best I could, following her directions as she moved about determining the priority of her patients' treatment based on the severity of their condition.

Although brutal, the attack had been short-lived. But every day was market day in Kintani and the centre had been filled with women shopping for whatever meagre supplies they could find at the stalls that lined the square. It was no more than a clearing, located close to the river so goods could be transferred to and fro – but it was probably the only space big enough to land a helicopter, and that had sealed the villagers' fate.

We counted twenty-seven dead, mostly women. There were babies and infants too, though no school-age children for they had been attending evening lessons at the other end of the town. With the help of the boat crew we dragged the dead to one side and covered them with blankets, plastic sheeting or whatever else we could find. Clusters of flies swarmed around us. Finally there were only eleven who Mariana decided she could treat, nine women, an infant and one old man.

'I have only a basic first-aid kit: morphine, bandages, IV fluids, and giving sets and cannulae, but it is not enough. Not enough of anything.' She went on talking as she worked. At no point did she pause or express the horror or the anger she must have been feeling. 'I can treat the peripheral injuries. They may survive if we can get them to a hospital with proper facilities. But the ones with chest and abdominal wounds - I can stop limbs bleeding by applying pressure but that's about all; control the pain and keep them hydrated – that is all I can do. They will die here. I will leave morphine with the school teacher. She will have to administer to them. We must get the others to a hospital where there are facilities.' She was having to make instant life or death decisions as she worked.

When Grant returned with the boat skipper, Marco was with them. They had further news. 'They've taken Nzinga,' Marco announced. 'And you know who was with them? Mendesa! The chopper landed here in the square. He asked where she was. Then she came forward. She was already in the square. She tried to reason with him. She wanted him to help ferry the wounded but he wasn't here for that. He threatened to shoot up the school if she didn't cooperate. So she went without resisting. What could she do? They hustled her on board and took off. There was no question of her opposing him.'

'What about medical supplies?' Mariana asked Marco, placing the immediate needs of her patients first.

'Nothing. There's a small clinic but no nurse, no supplies. They say she left a week ago to buy medicines in Kazunda City, but she has not returned.'

'I cannot do any more here now. We need to get the injured to hospital urgently,' Mariana said.

'Kazunda City?' I asked.

'I'm afraid so. With gunshot wounds it is not easy to see what damage has been done. But at some point we may have to accept that we just don't have the resources to treat these people. It will be a difficult journey but we will make them as comfortable as we can and I still have some opiates left.'

'There's only the launch, then the Land Rover,' I said. 'Let's get them down to the river.'

The townsfolk were in a state of shock but a few of the men helped us transfer the eleven injured to the launch on makeshift stretchers hastily fabricated out of bamboo and plastic sheeting. Finally, we got them down to the river and on board. Mariana had cleared room in the after cabin to create an improvised treatment centre. It was a cramped space with little ventilation. 'It will have to do,' she said.

'These people are asking us to find Nzinga,' said Marco pointing to the group of men who had helped us bring the injured to the riverside.

'Tell them we will find her and bring her to safety,' said Grant confidently. Marco translated but the men still looked anxious and confused. They didn't seem to share Grant's optimism.

CHAPTER 19

Only the skipper agreed to take us back down the river. The other two crewmen stayed behind. We cast off at midnight leaving the Kintani folk to mourn their dead and dying, and wondering how to cope without their leader. Marco, Grant and I took it in turns to relieve Mariana in tending to the injured and grabbing an hour or so of sleep when off duty. The next day as the sun reached and passed its zenith the heat became unbearable, the air humid and suffocating. Some of the injured were able to sit outside on the after-deck over which we had rigged a makeshift awning. It was the most comfortable space on the boat providing some shade and as we gathered speed the breeze created by the boat's movement gave some further respite. Others were too badly injured to be moved and it was these who Mariana paid closest attention to, and for whom she held out the least hope.

'In this climate I worry more about infection and disease than the injuries themselves,' she told me. 'Did you know that in the Crimean War Florence Nightingale observed that seventy percent of mortality was due to disease rather than injury from battle? It led to the setting up of the Army Medical Service, which was a great achievement.'

'I didn't know that.'

'She was my hero when I was training, a highly intelligent woman. She had friends in high places too and she used these people – politicians and all sorts – to get things done. She was a little obsessive you could say.'

We talked and sometimes dozed fitfully when and where we could throughout the long day. No one had eaten and water supplies were rationed, with the injured getting priority.

The baby died in the late afternoon, but its mother still cradled its shrunken little body in her arms while staring fixedly ahead. We didn't stop and by ten that evening, helped by the downstream current, we had moored at the village where we'd left the Land Rover and transferred the injured onto the bank. We said farewell to the launch skipper before he headed back up to Kintani, then helped Mariana prepare the wounded survivors for the five-hour road trip back to Kazunda City. Marco drove, this time with Grant and myself alongside him. Mariana squeezed into the back with the injured.

It was a hell of a journey and we stopped frequently so she could attend to her patients but the old man died when we were close to the city. We reached the hospital on the city's eastern outskirts at six the following morning, but any sense of relief was short-lived. The place was crowded with victims of the fighting that was raging across the city. The entrance, reception area and corridors were choked with people, many of them men in uniform seeking medical attention. The staff, clearly overwhelmed, were doing what they could. Grant and I waited by the Land Rover with our own small group of Kintani patients while Marco and Mariana went inside to get help.

I discovered a crate of water in plastic bottles round the back of the building and carried an armful back to share between them. Eventually Marco and Mariana returned with a doctor and nurse and two assistants pushing stretchers on trolleys. The medics both looked exhausted but were carrying first aid kits and set about attending to our patients out there in the open.

'They will take care of them now, as best they can,' said Mariana. She looked even more spent than the medics.

'What's going on in the city?' Grant asked.

'There is still widespread fighting between troops loyal to Loma and those who joined the mercenaries of Mendesa,' Marco replied. 'He promised them each a thousand-dollar bonus and better pay and conditions if they sided with him. And there are rumours that Loma is dead. Others say he is barricaded inside the Black Reef palace. No one knows for sure. Also I asked one soldier, an officer here who had been shot in the leg, why Mendesa would want to abduct Nzinga. He thought it was because he did not want to fight on two fronts. He was worried Nzinga would rally the people from the countryside behind her and march on the city before he had gained a grip on power. I don't know whether this is the only reason but that's what he thought.'

'Where is she now?'

'He didn't know what they've done with her. We asked about Cordeiro too but again he knew nothing.'

'So who's controlling the TV and radio stations?' Grant asked.

'Mendesa. He is broadcasting constantly saying he is in control of the city and that he will take the whole country within the next forty-eight hours.'

'And is he in control of the city?'

'The coastal strip and that northern flank around the police compound, yes. Now he is focused on dislodging the presidential guard from the palace. That's where the fighting is heaviest. But the situation is very fluid and confused. Not all the presidential guard will be loyal to one side or another. They may split. No one knows for sure what is happening.'

'Is the Portuguese Embassy accessible?' Grant asked him.

'I don't know. It's in the southern part of the city so maybe it is.'

'I want to get there. Mariana,' he called over to where

she was helping the medics and she came across.

'Come with me. You'll be safer at the embassy and we can find out what's happening. I need to establish some kind of official link with the outside world and the Portuguese are our best bet.'

'I have decided it is better I stay here with these people. They are my patients now.'

'I thought you were handing them over to the medics here. You can do more good from the embassy. Come with me now and you can return here later.'

'No, I've changed my mind. I will stay here now. What about you, Angus?' she asked deflecting attention away from herself.

'I need Marco to help me.'

Grant interjected: 'Help you do what? We need to stay together. Come to the embassy with me.'

'Best if you go, Grant, and do what you have to do. You don't need me there too.'

'What are you planning? Mount your own private assault on the palace? From the embassy we can call up military assistance from the Portuguese. They will have forces in the region.'

'Possibly, but it will take days to get political approval and prepare an offensive on a sovereign nation even if it was once their colony. They'd need a UN resolution before they could send their own troops in. We don't have time. If

Mendesa's on the verge of taking power we need to stop him, and we need to find Nzinga. That's what I'm going to do, with help from Marco here.'

I knew the odds were against us. If Loma was really dead it was only a matter of time before his regime and the infrastructure around it collapsed. Mendesa already had control of the TV and radio stations and his forces stood at the gates of the Black Reef palace. Meanwhile, he'd abducted Nzinga, and Cordeiro had disappeared.

'You're mad. I'm ordering you, Gus. Come with me.'

'You know me well enough, Grant. I'll be in touch.'

CHAPTER 20

'It will not be easy.'

'I didn't think it would be, Marco. But do you know how I can get in or not? I was thinking from the seaward side? What do you reckon?'

Over the past few days Marco had repeatedly demonstrated his resourcefulness. He was more than Mariana's sidekick, more than just a fixer. He had initiative and didn't wait to be told what to do. And I'd noticed how he'd grown into this role as each calamitous event followed the last. He was smart and physically tough; and above all Marco was a Kazundan patriot eager to see his country return to the peace and order he remembered from his youth, when Mariana's family had employed his parents in the family home and the two had been childhood playmates, growing up together. I'd spent a lot of time thinking how I could influence the outcome of these events which were largely out of our control and I'd concluded that I couldn't do a thing without Marco's help. But Marco wasn't a fool – and I knew that what I was planning was bordering on the reckless. He wouldn't be easily persuaded.

'They say there is a small harbour cut out of the rocks on the reef, and from there an entrance to the old fort, and to the palace itself,' he said. 'But it will be guarded of course. It would be very dangerous.'

'Dangerous but not impossible. I'm going to try it but I need your help. I need a few things.'

'Of course, you have my help. Tell me.'

I reeled off a list and he laughed. 'That is a long list! How do you expect me to find all this? And a gun too?'

'Marco, this man Mendesa, he's bad, really bad. You must have heard the stories about him. He'll wreak chaos and destruction on your country. He'll drain the nation's coffers and the people will starve. Worse than Loma even. Is that what you want? If we can find Nzinga, help to instate her and undermine or remove Mendesa, then we have a chance to bring some stability to the country.'

'You make it sound straightforward. I think your boss was right, you are mad. Even if you find her she's as big a threat to Mendesa as she was to Loma. He'll never negotiate with her. Mr Douglas is seeing the ambassador. Perhaps he can help.'

'How can he? It's like I said, the Portuguese will never intervene militarily. They have a history of bad experiences in their African colonies made worse by their failed military campaigns. So how? Diplomatic intervention? The UN? Come on.'

'Mr Douglas told me the Americans, the CIA, would help overthrow Mendesa.'

'Well that didn't work out, did it? Mendesa and his friends blew the CIA's offshore base to hell. Anyway, we don't have time to stand here arguing. Can you find me the items on this list or not?'

'Okay, if you are so determined I will see what I can do. I'll need a few hours. Meet me here at nine o'clock tonight.'

'Thanks, Marco,' I said as he headed off towards the Land Rover. Then he stopped and turned back to me. 'Let's make it happen, Mr Gus!'

There wasn't much I could do before then so I went into the hospital to find Mariana and offer what little help I could.

***

It took us three hours to drive from the hospital. The city was in a state of chaos. Crowds jammed the streets and the white Land Rover with its UN markings attracted unwanted attention. At one point we were stopped at a police cordon. A fierce argument ensued which Marco was determined to win and in the end they let us through.

'We're UN personnel, right?' he said to me. Then we saw why the police hadn't wanted us to pass. A few hundred yards ahead was a crowd of young men armed with stones, sticks, Molotov cocktails and the odd machete. They'd formed themselves into a loose line and were heading towards the police barricade. And we were in between the two.

'Keep driving,' I said. 'They'll move out of the way.' And they did, but only after a lot of shouting and banging on the windows of the Land Rover. Two of them climbed onto the roof. It was a flashpoint waiting to explode and we were lucky to get through. Our route was less charged after that and Marco would stop and talk to small clusters of people to find out what he could about the situation in the city, which was rapidly descending into anarchy.

Marco had found what he could from my list and, despite my efforts to dissuade him, insisted on coming with me. But he had news: 'I have spoken to a friend, Hugo. He is a junior officer in the presidential guard. They are supposed to be an elite unit but they haven't been paid for six months. He says there is much discontent among the officers and other ranks. He has offered to help us.'

'Discontent with whom? Loma, Mendesa …?'

'Both. He says he and his colleagues are all sick of the nepotism, the corruption. It's not what they trained for, to serve these dictators.'

'Can we trust him?'

'Yes, we can trust him, I am sure of that, and it was he who gave me the gun and ammunition.'

It was approaching midnight by the time we waded into the water from a beach to the north of Black Reef. We were wearing snorkels, masks, fins and black wetsuits that had belonged to a couple of surfers Marco knew. They were old, the rubber was worn and had lost much of its elasticity after years of exposure to sun and seawater, but they were black and would provide some protection from the sharp basalt of the reef. And we carried waterproof bags with dry clothing and, in mine, the gun.

The water wasn't cold but I could see in the distance there was a heavy swell breaking over the reef. We swam some way out to sea then arced in towards the reef and the white surf. The harbour lay ahead of us now and as I crested each wave I could see it was well protected by breakwaters either side of the entrance. As we got closer I saw a large boat moored alongside the quay inside the harbour.

Using our snorkels now we swam as far as the break-waters and, taking our time, peered round into the harbour. It looked deserted and we swam on in. Marco found an iron ladder attached to the harbour wall and we climbed up onto the quayside. The boat was more than just a gin palace. I'd seen these things in the hands of shipowners and oligarchs cruising around the Aegean. It was a forty-metre motor yacht designed to look like a small naval warship, its grey hull and superstructure giving it an intentionally menacing appearance.

I looked at the waterproof watch Marco had acquired. We were seven minutes early for our rendezvous with Hugo so had time for a look around. The harbour had been hewn out of the basalt rock; it would have been a gruelling task, and it didn't look like it had been done recently. The boat itself was moving awkwardly against its heavy-duty fenders. I could see from the satcom domes, radomes and antennae sprouting from the mast that it was equipped for long-distance voyages. It was moored facing seaward, for a speedy getaway I mused, and looked well-maintained.

'Was this one of Loma's toys or has Mendesa brought it with him?' I asked Marco.

'It must be Loma's, but I don't know where he got it from.'

We found the entrance to the fort, a watertight door set into the rock face. Pushing the dog handle up I pulled it open and waited, gun in hand. Hugo appeared dressed in military fatigues and looking anxious. He was young, tall and skinny.

'Come, quickly,' he said.

We headed inside. Ahead of us was a long corridor with a flight of steps at the end. It was a damp place. The once-white plaster was flaking from the rock walls and water dripped from the ceiling. At the foot of the steps Hugo halted. 'I will go first. Then if all is okay I will flash my torch down at you – three times, like this,' he said, demonstrating.

He turned and headed up the steps. As I'd hoped, this

was the safest way to enter the fort he assured us, and also that the presidential household and the guards who were on duty in the palace were holed up in the eastern wing on the landward side of the fort. It seemed a long wait, but after ten minutes we saw the flashes from his torch. He left it switched on then so we could see our way. At the top of the steps we went through another steel door and down another corridor. At the end of this one, we passed through yet another door into the kitchens, and beyond that up more stairs, which led into a huge dining hall.

Now I began to sense the atmosphere inside the palace itself. Here, little remained of the original Portuguese fort. Loma had converted this old citadel into every African despot's idea of how to demonstrate his power and wealth while at the same time managing to make it look painfully kitsch. And pervading it all was an atmosphere of decay. The salt air from the ocean had crept into the place, rotting away at concrete, mortar and fabrics. Even the light switches and electrical wiring were oxidising. But as we moved closer to the eastern wing the ambience changed to a more lived-in look; until we came to another hall, this one resembling a meeting room dominated by a long ebony table with matching chairs and a huge portrait of Eduardo Loma hanging at one end of the room. But that wasn't what caught my eye, for directly beneath and to one side of the picture, spread across the wall, was a messy splatter of dried blood. And on the cheetah-skin rug beneath the painting was more blood, which had stained parts of the animal skin so dark as to be almost black.

'Loma,' whispered Hugo. 'This is where they killed him – with machetes.' He drew a finger across his throat. Throughout his thirty-two year reign as president, Loma had both emulated and mocked his neighbour in the Democratic Republic of the Congo, Joseph-Désiré Mobutu. While Mobuto sported a leopard-skin hat, Loma chose one of cheetah skin, saying the cheetah ran at twice the speed of a leopard. Clearly, he'd carried the metaphor through to the palace furnishings. Ironic, I thought, that in his dying moments, he had collapsed onto the very symbol he'd chosen to signify his power and supremacy.

'Who killed him?' I asked.

'The presidential guard. It was the officers who did it.'

'His death is no loss to our nation,' Marco said. 'Now we must find Mendesa, and Nzinga.'

As he spoke, like a scene from a Victorian drawing-room drama, a figure appeared from a doorway in the far corner of the hall.

'Welcome to Black Reef,' said Carlos Cordeiro. 'I might be able to help you there.'

CHAPTER 21

'What the hell are you doing here?' I asked, instinctively pointing the gun at his chest.

'I could ask you the same question, Angus McKinnon. Come through and let's have a drink.' He gestured to the door through which he'd entered. 'Your friends are welcome to stay although this isn't the safest place in Kazunda right now.'

I turned to Marco and Hugo. 'Go now.' I said. 'I'll catch up with you later.'

'Shouldn't we wait here?' Marco said doubtfully.

I turned to them and gripped Marco's hand. 'Marco, you've both been great. Now go, and watch out for yourselves.' They didn't need more urging.

I followed Cordeiro into a lavishly furnished room. On the white marble floor was a huge golden silk rug on which was set a three-piece Chesterfield suite upholstered in a gold-effect faux leather. Around the room's perimeter was set an assortment of reproduction Louis XIV tables and

199

chairs. I didn't bother to inspect the incongruous gilt-framed paintings of horses rearing up in long-forgotten battles, which hung around the walls. The room was lit by a huge chandelier which flickered with the erratic electricity supply, another metaphor for everything that was rotten with the place. The overall effect was of fading ostentation. Cordeiro poured us both whiskies from a crystal decanter. 'Sit down,' he said gesturing to the suite and handing me a glass. 'Don't mind the opulence.'

I was still wearing the wetsuit, dripping seawater onto the silk rug. I took a long drink and sat down in one of the wing chairs. 'I was hoping to find Mendesa,' I said. 'I didn't expect you to be here.'

'Find Mendesa and what? Shoot him with that antique you're carrying? A Browning Hi-Power is it not? They are common in these parts. First adopted by Belgium for military service over eighty years ago; and that's an early model. An original P-35 if I'm not wrong: one of the most influential pistols in the history of small arms. Did you know Colonel Gaddafi had one? They found it on him when they dragged him out of that drain a few years ago. But yours? Perhaps worth more at auction than what you might be using it for. I can find you something more effective if you'd like?'

'I'm told it's in good working order,' I said, still pointing it at him. 'Now just tell me what your part is in all this, Cordeiro. Just who's side are you backing?'

'I can understand why you are here and I will lay my cards on the table. But just so you know, Mendesa seized Nzinga. He commandeered a helicopter from the army and one of his mercenaries flew it up to her base at Kintani. Mendesa himself fired into the crowd there. And I would help you find Mendesa to do with as you would wish. I would pull the trigger for you. But he has gone.'

'What do you mean he's gone?'

'Events have been moving fast in the last few hours. Your friend from the presidential guard told you about the assassination of Loma but he may not have heard what has been happening in the city these last few hours, and here at the fort.

'Mendesa was smart, or he thought he was. He already had his own local militia in the city: a private force of loyal thugs drawn mostly from the army's ranks and the poorest neighbourhoods. They were promised land and cash payments in dollars. They were promised power and influence. So they were already standing by awaiting his orders.

'Mendesa knew that the presidential guard had killed Loma but he broadcast to his followers that he personally had struck the fatal blow. Then he and his mercenaries marshalled the local insurgents together and ordered them to kill anyone they suspected of being loyal to Loma; and anyone who challenged his own right to take power. And he told them they were at liberty to rape the women and their daughters. Rape is an established weapon of war as you know. By forcing a young woman to bear the enemy's child they spread fear and the community is then easier to control.

'But let me tell you something else about Mendesa that you may not know. I do know him. He is entirely unpredictable but for a reason, because by this means he encourages uncertainty and he uses this to assert control. He is outwardly smooth and sophisticated, but he's a sadist and a psychopath. He is without empathy or compassion. I'll give you an example. They say he enjoys watching prostitutes being murdered while having sex. He arranges these things for his own pleasure. It didn't surprise me at all that he chose to fly up to Kintani, not just to grab Nzinga, but for the pleasure of slaughtering those people. He is truly evil.

'But just like Loma, Mendesa underestimated the presidial guard and where their loyalties lie. So things didn't go according to plan.'

'Go on,' I said as he paused to drink his whisky.

'Mendesa's mercenaries were already advancing on the palace. They encountered the guard. There was a firefight. There were heavy losses on both sides, but the mercenaries were outnumbered and wiped out - to the last man, I am told.'

'Where is Mendesa now then?'

'He has fled. But I fear he will return one day. When the guard had wiped out the mercenaries they went after

Mendesa's militia, the insurgents I mentioned. The guard quickly outgunned them, most of them anyway. They weren't well organised and were poorly armed. So apart from a few pockets of resistance the guard are pretty much in control, at least in the city, and at least for now.'

'And Nzinga?'

'Ah, Nzinga. She is safe now and I will open the way for her to take power, but I have a favour to ask.'

'You can influence that? You are close to her, I've heard, but do you have the guard with you?'

'The guard is loyal to Nzinga. They see her as I do and since you are here, I suspect as you do too. They see her as the nation's hope. And remember, the presidential guard is an elite force drawn from a military academy which was established by the Portuguese before independence. They are educated and they are united. And they know the meaning and the importance of loyalty.'

'And now they await Nzinga?'

'That's right.'

'I understand why they would be loyal to Nzinga, but where do you fit in?'

'They know that I have brought Nzinga to this point. You may see me as some Machiavellian *éminence grise*. Perhaps I am a king maker, or a queen maker, but I assure you my motives are unselfish. First though, this favour, a demand even, for you to put to my old comrade-in-arms, Grant Douglas.'

'Tell me.'

'I want him to arrange asylum for me. I want full and permanent immunity from prosecution and lifetime protection from the American security services; an annual income of one hundred thousand dollars plus an initial payment of two million dollars for the purchase of an apartment in the city of San Francisco.' Clearly he'd been rehearsing it all.

'Forgive me for reminding you of this,' I said, 'but as I understand it, by your part in bringing down Loma you've just aided and abetted the killing of a platoon of Navy SEALS, a team of CIA agents and specialists, and the crew of a US-owned oil rig. Do you really think Grant Douglas will want to do business with you now?'

He spoke vehemently: 'No! Believe me, I didn't know that's what they'd do. They gave no indication that thy would attack the floatel. But Loma's regime had to fall. Don't you see? Loma had to be stopped to give this country a chance. I know you understand that, otherwise you wouldn't have risked your life coming here tonight. And that meant stopping the CIA's support for him.'

'So you're not denying that you tipped your Russian friends off as to the real purpose of the *Sea-En Resolution*. And that that tip-off led to them launching the attack, from one of their subs out there in the Atlantic I presume. So I doubt very much whether either Langley, or the Brits for that matter, would accede to your request.'

'Britain? Are you joking? Put me in one of your safe houses and you might as well announce it on Russian TV. Listen, it is your friend Grant Douglas who we're talking about here. He's CIA. We know each other from Laos. Speak to him. But in case he thinks I have nothing to offer in return, tell him this too: in return for my asylum terms being met I will share everything I know about Russia's strategic aims on the continent of Africa. And I'm not talking about what's in the public domain.'

I looked across at him, sitting relaxed in his white shirt, cream slacks and loafers, a master of playing one side against the other. 'You're a cool one, aren't you,' I said. 'I will speak to him, but he too will have to consult. And you had better give him a taste of what you're offering.'

'Of course. And then we will wait while he consults with his masters in Langley.'

'It could take days, weeks even to get such an arrangement set up.'

'I fear time is not on our side. If the Americans want their flow of Kazunda's oil to continue they must be seen to be supporting Nzinga. Mendesa has fled and Loma is dead. The king is dead, long live the queen.'

'You've masterminded this from the beginning haven't you.'

'No, not quite. Acquiring the materiel in Trabzon, chartering the *Dalmatia Star*: that was all arranged by Mendesa working directly with the GRU. The Russians didn't want their own equipment and people showing up here so having Mendesa as their proxy suited them nicely. But yes, above all of that, I was preparing Nzinga for her accession. That is all that matters now.'

'So you had the presidential guard on side from the start.'

'It was a cornerstone of the plan. It wouldn't have worked without them.'

'Did Nzinga know?'

'No. I had to keep the details from her for security reasons. I just promised I would make it possible – for the good of the nation. She trusted me. In Angola I saw how civil war between different factions tore the country apart – the Cubans and South Africans all fighting as proxies for the Russians and Americans. Here we will avoid that. And Nzinga is the only person who can unite Kazunda now.'

'How did you get the Russians to trust you, and make them believe you were supporting them and Mendesa against Loma while your real agenda was to crush them both in favour of Nzinga? Seems like a risky strategy – weren't you afraid they'd sniff out your true motive? And what do you think they'll do now they know you double-crossed them?'

'The Russians were happy to trust me. They knew I'd fallen out with the CIA years ago and they bought into my support for a coup in Kazunda. I introduced them to Mendesa and the pieces fell into place after that.'

'So Mendesa was a stooge, a useful idiot?'

'Not exactly. The Russians saw him as their stalking horse – a means to an end. But Mendesa himself? He was ambitious and hungry for power - for his own sake. And I am sure he still is.'

'Where is he now?' I asked again.

'I understand he was flown out of the country this morning.'

'Did you know in advance he was escaping?'

'If I had known I would have stopped him. But I wasn't surprised. He's a coward. Once his mercenaries were finished and he saw the presidential guard was siding with Nzinga, he gave up and fled.'

'Where was he taken?'

'Pointe-Noire.'

'And from there?'

'I don't know. Back to Zurich perhaps. Or into hiding somewhere. He has many enemies now.'

'Did Mendesa order the murder of Captain Babic on the *Dalmatia Star*?'

'I suppose he would have condoned it. He was working with the GRU and their man Horvat. They needed to remove anyone who presented a threat, and the captain was one of those threats. He didn't like what was happening on his ship.'

'So Horvat and Mendesa were working together?'

'Yes, they worked together but that is not to say they were allies, let alone friends. Horvat was the GRU's man there to protect Russia's interests.'

'I see. And where is Nzinga now?'

'She is safe. The guard freed her and took her to São Gabriel island off the coast from here. Don't worry, the guard are loyal to her. They are there protecting her. They trust her to do what is right for the country.'

'I don't understand why you want to go to the US,' I said. 'Surely with your Marxist ideology you'd rather see this thing through; work with Nzinga to make it happen?'

'I'm getting old. I want to experience some of the good life before my time is up. And I'm tired of this country, and of Africa. My satisfaction will be seeing her installed. I know her well. She will succeed and she doesn't need me now.'

When Grant and I had discussed it back on the river, we were pretty close to the truth: Cordeiro was a clever sonofabitch alright. He'd manipulated events to suit his own ends, though I doubted whether he'd still be on Grant's Christmas card list, or his masters' in the GRU, after all this. But although I'd never met Nzinga, from everything I'd heard about her she would make an infinitely better leader than either Loma or Mendesa, so I couldn't disagree with Cordeiro's vision. His methods were unorthodox but in the end his aims were altruistic.

He went over to a table and picked up a satellite phone.

'Here, call Douglas.'

I called the last number Grant had given me. It went to voicemail and I left a message, giving him the number to call me back on. 'He was going to the Portuguese Embassy,' I said. 'Can you get hold of the ambassador?'

'Let's try,' he said. I handed back the phone and after a while he got through. It was three-thirty in the morning. We'd been talking for hours yet I had no idea what was going on now in the city. He spoke rapidly in Portuguese then said, 'Douglas is there. They will wake him.'

There was another delay until they got hold of him. 'Grant, I have your colleague with me.' He handed me the phone and I sketched out Cordeiro's conditions.

'Gus, we're calling up a squad of Portuguese commandos to storm the palace. How do you want to play this?'

'Too late, Grant. Stand them down. Things have been moving fast here.' And I described the events that had unfolded in the last few hours as Cordeiro had related them. 'If you're in favour of his proposal we can work this out. Mendesa's gone now. And I imagine this intel that Cordeiro's offering on Russia's Africa strategy could be of value. It's your call. Have the commandos on standby off the coast and get Langley, or whoever you talk to, on the phone if that's what you want to do, not forgetting his part in blowing your rig to kingdom come of course,' I added, putting the phone onto speaker. 'The situation is still fluid here but

Cordeiro's saying he has the presidential guard on side and Nzinga waiting in the wings. The guard will follow Nzinga, Grant. And the army will follow the guard,' Cordeiro interrupted stepping over to be closer to the phone. 'Mendesa is gone and has no local support here now.'

'Yeah, got it. What kind of intel are we talking about, Carlos? I need to feed my people some red meat.'

'In order for the coup to succeed, the GRU gave me access to certain information. The Russians are already training the special forces of many African nations, and equipping their armies. This you will know. But I have full details of these programmes and confidential files describing the Kremlin's future agenda: how they will empower certain governments and disrupt others. Their aspirations here in Kazunda are an example, but they have failed. The true extent of these Russian security deals is difficult for you to assess because you don't have access. They told me you don't and they seemed very certain about it. But to give you an idea, in at least one case, an African country's civilian intelligence agency was forced to spy on its own military counterpart just to figure out what kind of surveillance system they had bought from the Russians for a hundred million dollars, and how much of that found its way back to the generals. That's the kind of specifics I'm offering. There is much more but first I need your assurances. And Grant,' he added. 'I swear blind I didn't know they'd blow that rig up.'

'So what did you think they'd do? Invite everyone round for tea? Anyhow, leave it with me. Give me twelve hours to set something up. I'll get back to you.' He hung up.

'Okay,' I said. 'If you're in control you need to freeze the situation until this evening. You've got Nzinga safe; the police, the army, the presidential guard all on side. You can hold things as they are?'

'I will reassure them. They will wait.'

'And what will you do if Langley can't meet your conditions?'

'They will.'

CHAPTER 22

Cordeiro had taken up residence in Loma's palace apartments and showed me where I could shower and change into the clothes I'd stuffed into my waterproof bag. I rejoined him for the first reasonable meal I'd had in days: scrambled eggs, fruit juice and coffee. It went some way to fighting off the exhaustion that was washing over me in waves.

As we'd talked I'd found myself conflicted over my opinion of the man. I couldn't ignore his role in the destruction of the *Sea-En Resolution*. Did I believe him when he said he had not anticipated that his actions could have such devastating consequences? I wasn't sure. But there was something I had to respect about Carlos Cordeiro. He was a maverick, an anti-Establishment rebel, but above all he saw what needed to be done, what he believed in. He had principles and acted upon them rather than just tolerating the iniquities of those around him.

Breakfast was interrupted by the phone. It was Grant.

'Listen to this,' he said, speaking to me. 'There's no love

lost between Carlos Cordeiro and the CIA, but hey, surprise surprise, they've agreed to his demands. They say it's on the basis of what he's doing in bringing peace and democracy to Kazunda. That's horseshit. What they really want is to debrief him. They need more intel on Russia's plans in Africa. So he'd better produce the goods or the debriefing could last forever – you know what I mean? He could be detained for months or years. And they'll always have the option of calling him up in future. So there are strings attached, but if he's as good as his word, for now he can look forward to life as a sleeper in sunny San Francisco. I'll let you tell him the good news.'

'What about his role in the attack on the floatel?'

'They're pragmatic. He's got what they want. That intel he's offering is pure gold.'

'He may not believe it. I'm not sure I do.'

'He'll believe it because he wants to believe it.'

I walked out of the room, closing the door behind me. I was back in the hall where Loma had met his end. 'You know what, Grant? I'm not in any way defending what he did, but Cordeiro's an idealist. Maybe he wasn't back in Laos or Angola but he's seen the light now. He wants to have played his part in creating a stable nation out of chaos. I think he's seeking redemption.' I didn't need to remind Grant of his own culpability in the affair either.

'You're giving him a lot of credit, buddy. He knows as

well as you and I that this is all just a replay of the Cold War in Southeast Asia and Angola. It was never about ideology then and it isn't now. It's about power through control and influence: control of Africa's minerals and its oil and gas: by Russia, by China, by us. Tell him he's got his wish, and he can trust us against his GRU pals any day.'

I went back in and conveyed the news to Cordeiro. 'I will need a visa, new documents,' was his first reaction.

'You'll get all that. They'll put the process in motion. First though, Nzinga. I must talk to her.'

'You shall. It is time for her to return.' He stood, and headed for the door.

'Wait,' I said. 'We'll go to this island together.'

'You don't trust me?'

'I don't know you.'

He laughed. 'Very well, we shall go together. I hope you don't suffer from seasickness. It's rough out there.'

*****

Dawn was breaking as Cordeiro manoeuvred the boat out of the hidden harbour and into open waters. As we headed into the Atlantic swell he moved the revs up until we were cutting through the waves at twenty knots, with shipped water crashing across the deck. We turned north in the direction of São Gabriel and the line of Sea-En rigs came into view, spaced out across the ocean, their cranes, flare stacks and towers lit up against the sky. We passed the grotesque, blackened wreck of the *Sea-En Resolution* protruding from the water like the work of some mad sculptor. Sooner or later there'd have to be a massive clean-up operation to remove it.

'How long have you worked for Grant Douglas?' he asked without turning his attention from the sea ahead.

'I don't really work for him – I'm a freelance insurance investigator,' I said. 'I have my own claims handling business in Greece. Much of my work is done on behalf of the Caledonian Marine Mutual. Grant is CEO there.'

He looked across at me. 'Why the pretence all of a sudden?'

'Because that's the way it is, Carlos. This escapade is something I got dragged into. Not for the first time, but it's not my usual line of work, believe me.' He looked sceptical.

'For an aircraft pilot you handle a boat well,' I said, changing the subject.

'Yeah, in Laos and 'Nam we got to do pretty much everything.'

'Grant told me you went bamboo. What was that all about?'

'I liked it out there. Okay, it was war. We were bombing the shit out of the place but it was a big adrenalin rush the whole time. Sure, I went bamboo - found myself a nice little local girl and shacked up with her. She was a Hmong – they were the local hill tribe in those parts and were fighting alongside us like tigers. But I was a pilot first and foremost. And Air America was kinda loosely structured, the Ravens too. We had a lot of latitude when it came to how we lived our lives. We were paramilitaries as well as pilots and I found myself feeding intel back to the CIA station chief in Vientiane. That's how I met Grant. He was a junior intelligence officer reporting to the station chief so I saw a lot of him.'

'That boat – the Navy PCF we hitched a lift on?'

'Yeah, when Laos was wound up I stuck around for a while. Then Ailani died.' He stopped talking and raised a pair of powerful binoculars to his eyes. 'See ahead?' he said passing me the glasses. 'São Gabriel.'

I looked through them and saw the island, a black rock sticking out of the ocean, surrounded by white surf.

I handed the glasses back to him. 'You were saying.'

'Yeah, when she died that was hard. I bummed around for a while then headed for Angola. Pretty soon I realised that those PCFs would be ideal on the rivers there and up the coast. So they shipped half a dozen over. When I came up here to Kazunda I brought one with me.'

It took us another forty minutes to reach the island. He brought us into the harbour, even less spacious than the one at Black Reef, with the same cautious expertise I'd noticed when he flew us from Pointe-Noire.

I jumped ashore to secure the mooring lines and looked around. There was a concrete shed on the quayside and that was about it. São Gabriel was a miserable looking place hardly worth calling an island. The constant battering it took from the ocean created a thick, salt-laden mist that hung over the place, making the air dank and clammy. Two men in military fatigues and wearing the maroon berets of the presidential guard approached us and greeted Cordeiro with noticeable deference. The three of them conferred between themselves before he turned back to me.

'She's well,' he announced. 'Come. Time for you to meet her.'

We walked up a narrow unpaved track running into the interior. Despite the salt spray the island was thick with veg-etation resilient to the briny environment. After a mile or so the track petered out and we came to another concrete hut, rotting and green with mould. Sitting outside on a rickety old chair was Nzinga.

I had imagined a robust, forceful woman resembling Winnie Mandela in her younger days. The two had nothing in common. Nzinga stood up and went straight to Cordeiro. They embraced, and after some time she held him at arm's length as if inspecting him, or to remind herself of what he looked like. They spoke intently to each other in Portu-guese. Then Cordeiro turned to me and introduced us. We shook hands.

She was in her mid to late thirties. Although petite, she radiated energy through her gestures and body language, and I sensed determination in her manner. Something about her reminded me of Mariana.

'Carlos tells me you and Mariana Da Cunha helped my people in Kintani. How many died, do you know?'

'Almost thirty in the attack when you were taken, plus those who didn't survive the journey to the city.'

She shook her head. 'So senseless. I could not resist them when they came for me.'

'I understand Mendesa was the one who fired from the helicopter.'

'Yes, it was Mendesa. He treated it like a sport. That man is a psychopath. I knew he saw me as a threat to his plan to take over the presidency but I went willingly. I thought it would stop the slaughter of my people. He threatened to kill the children in the school if I didn't go with him.' She shook her head. 'And Carlos tells me he has left the country; run like the coward he is.'

She hesitated before switching her attention. 'And what about you and this other man – Mr Douglas?'

'Are you asking what we are doing in your country?'

'Yes, I would like to know that.'

'It will take some time.'

'Explain it on the way back to Black Reef,' said Cordeiro. 'I have told her you will not oppose the changes that are coming. We must go now.'

'I'll explain,' I said, 'and you must also speak with Grant Douglas and Mariana da Cuhna.'

As we walked back to the boat they talked excitedly to each other in Portuguese. This time the two guards cast off and joined us on board as Cordeiro manoeuvred out of the little harbour. I moved back to where Nzinga was sitting on a bench at the back of the wheelhouse, the two guards standing nearby. I sat down next to her as we headed back into the ocean's swell.

'I hate boats,' she said. 'I don't trust them and they make me ill. Aircraft I don't mind.'

'Have you travelled much?'

'In Africa, yes; and to Portugal where I studied.'

'Are you confident of your revolution succeeding?'

'Of course. It will be the Mussaenda Revolution, called after our national flower, and symbolising peace. You know Portugal had its Carnation Revolution – it was mostly peaceful and brought big changes to that country, for the better. This is what we will have here now.'

'And your system of government?'

'You know we are Marxists, but I am pragmatic and flexible. I studied politics and economics. I know which systems have worked and which have failed. Do I expect to turn Kazunda into some kind of economic miracle? Of course not. Marx was a moralist, not an economist. I know that. But

I promise we will share the country's wealth with its people. And we will not tolerate the kind of corruption and cronyism that we have suffered from all these years. Ours will be an honest and fair government.'

'Will you have elections?'

'Only when the time is right. When we have rid ourselves of the corrupt patronage we see in so many of our neighbouring countries, where politicians buy blocks of votes with promises of future favours.'

'I wish you well,' I said.

'Thank you. Now it is my turn to ask you some questions.'

But Nzinga's turn never came.

'Let's stand,' I said as the swell surged. 'It will be more comfortable. Keep your eyes on the horizon.' We stood with our backs braced against the bulkhead, our feet planted wide apart as the boat lurched from wave to wave.

We were no more than three hundred yards off the wreck of the *Sea-En Resolution* when the bullets struck, smashing through the glass and striking Cordeiro first in his shoulder then his neck. At first he held onto the wheel to support himself. Then he turned to us, his eyes locking onto Nzinga. She screamed and threw herself towards him. More rounds crashed into the wheelhouse as he fell to the deck, still gripping the wheel. The boat veered in response, turning wildly in a tight circle. I dived across the deck and grabbed the wheel, forcing it back into the forward position. I glanced up to see where we were heading – straight towards the rig. I looked down at where Cordeiro lay, Nzinga draped across him. He was bleeding heavily from the wound in his neck. I turned the wheel again to get back on course, almost losing my balance as I slipped in a pool of his blood. Now we were leaving the rig behind us and the wheelhouse was protected from the line of fire. I held the boat on course for Black Reef. I could see it clearly now, its profile protruding from the coast and surrounded by the crashing surf.

***

I never knew for certain who killed Carlos Cordeiro. It had to be a trained sniper, equipped, I guessed, with laser rangefinder, meteorological measuring equipment, ballistic prediction software and God knows what else to get that kind of accuracy. It was a professional hit alright and the assassin had fired from the *Sea-En Resolution*, American-owned but now an abandoned hulk. It wouldn't have been difficult to get onboard and set up a firing position. But the shooter would have to have known that Cordeiro was going to pass within shooting distance. The CIA had good reason to do away with him. No matter what his excuses, Cordeiro had, initially at least and arguably for what he saw as the greater good, sided with Mendesa and the Russians to bring about

Loma's downfall. And to achieve that he had informed them of the CIA operations base on board the *Sea-En Resolution*. Many US citizens had died because of it. Neither would Grant have mourned his death for Grant had been complicit in revealing to Cordeiro the CIA's plans to protect Loma from the coup in the first place. I wondered whether the CIA had ever seriously intended to accede to Cordeiro's asylum request.

Then again, Cordeiro had also abandoned Mendesa and his Russian-backed coup in favour of Nzinga's cause, providing ample motive for the GRU to eliminate him as well. He'd double-crossed the Americans, the Russians and Mendesa to ensure Nzinga's accession. Whichever side had carried out the hit, Cordeiro had paid the price for his own double dealings. Mariana had been right when she'd said perhaps he'd been too clever for his own good. Either way, it had been one hell of a shot.

Nzinga wept as she cradled his lifeless body in her arms. The two guards had stationed themselves on the companionway outside the wheelhouse, scanning the sea for further threats. Had one or both of them betrayed Cordeiro by telling his killers when and where to attack? I'd never know. But I wondered how safe Nzinga was now without her champion.

I took the boat back into Black Reef's harbour and as one of the guards jumped ashore to take the lines I killed the engines and turned to Nzinga.

'Who?' she cried, but I didn't have an answer for her.

Instead I said, 'You cannot let this upset your plans, Nzinga.' I wasn't about to tell her that her comrade-in-arms had just requested asylum in the US, and was going to desert her. It didn't matter anyway.

She stared back at me, but after a while she got to her feet. 'I will go on,' she said. Then she sighed and I sensed she was already resigning herself to what had just happened. 'You know, we were once lovers; that was long ago. But we both believed in the cause. I will not lose faith now. And I will fulfil his dream. It is my dream too. *A luta continua!*'

She was more composed now. 'Loma and Mendesa respectively were each proxies for the American and Russian governments,' she said. 'Carlos knew the only way to bring peace and stability to the people of Kazunda was to make sure both of them failed. He knew that meant playing dirty but he will be honoured in my country as a true martyr to our cause.'

CHAPTER 23

Three days later Nzinga stepped out to meet her people. It was more a coronation than an inauguration. As she'd hoped, the revolution had been short-lived. What took place was a largely peaceful assignment of power to fill the vacuum left by Loma's assassination and the coup attempt. The police, the army and the presidential guard had, for now at least, supported the transition. They'd have been fools not too. Tens of thousands of citizens were out on the streets with their pink and white Mussaenda flowers and the crowds were swelling by the hour as others poured in from the countryside to join them. The atmosphere was peaceful for now, but febrile with excitement at the same time.

I joined Grant, Mariana and Marco along with the Portuguese ambassador and his staff to watch the spectacle from a balcony in one of the government buildings in the central square. But before Nzinga was presented, there was an important symbolic act to be performed. Inspired no doubt by events in Baghdad fifteen years earlier, a team of presidential guard officers and men climbed up the forty-foot bronze statue of Eduardo Loma and attached a heavy chain round its neck. Amidst a roar from the crowd the other end of the chain was attached to the tow-bar of an old armoured personnel carrier which Grant informed me was a Portuguese VBR Pandur. And so Loma was toppled. The crowd, frenzied now as the statue crashed to the ground, converged around it. Some attacked it with hammers, others just used sticks. As the crowd grew the police moved in to disperse them with batons, lashing out indiscriminately.

Just as it threatened to turn into a violent riot Nzinga's voice sounded across the square. '*Pare! Ele se foi!*'

Mariana translated: 'She's telling them to stop. He's gone.'

Nzinga was standing on the balcony from where, only days earlier, Loma had stood, ranting with threats of imprisonment or execution against those who would challenge his rule.

Her voice was restrained, her tone measured and with frequent pauses. She knew the gravity of her situation and she knew instinctively how to draw the crowd together. They stood in rapt silence, mesmerised. She was flanked by her closest advisors, mostly elders from the country's hinterland settlements, villages, townships, and from the city: thirty or so men and women in whose hands, along with their new president's, the future of the nation now rested. The swearing in of her cabinet was to take place immediately after the investiture ceremony, she said. There was to be little fanfare. She spoke of her plans and hopes for the future. And she paid tribute to Carlos Cordeiro. Her tone and manner conveyed a hands-on approach. And for now she had the nation eating out of her hand. They hung on her every word as her voice carried with an echo through loudspeakers, across the square packed with hopeful and eager Kazundans, their faces turned up towards her.

After it was all over we returned to Mariana's house on the hill. It was less than two weeks since we'd last sat around her stove discussing our plans, though it seemed much longer. Marco had gone to his family to continue the celebrations. Now there were just the three of us and Mariana prepared a simple meal herself which we ate on the veranda.

'What will you do?' I asked her. 'Are you staying on here?'

'No. There is nothing for me here, and I am happy to leave now I believe there is a future for Kazunda.'

Grant said, 'Nzinga has told you, you are welcome to stay.'

'I know. And I shall return from time to time I hope, but my life is in Lisbon.'

Grant smiled. 'From where there are direct flights to and from Edinburgh.'

She looked at him fondly. 'You know you will always be welcome, both of you.'

Grant took a drink of his Aguardente de Medronhos. 'There are loose ends to be tied up, many of them, Gus. We're not done yet.'

'I'll take care of them. You take care of Langley.'

'Hey, thanks!'

'You're welcome.'

Then he turned back to Mariana: 'Will you do one thing before you leave here? Will you tell Nzinga that she need not worry about Mendesa; about him returning to disrupt her rule and drag this country back into chaos and misery? Tell her we will take care of Mendesa.'

She nodded. 'And if you don't, then I will.'

CHAPTER 24

I left Kazunda the next morning, hitching a ride on one of Sea-En's Pilatus Porters to Pointe-Noire and from there on Air Maroc back to Casablanca. Pedro had messaged me from Lisbon saying I should visit the Club's representatives in the Moroccan city to discover the fate of the *Dalmatia Star*. I went straight from the airport to the offices of Ben-jelloun & Partners, a small and respected maritime law firm I'd had dealings with in the past.

'Welcome, old friend,' said Rachid Benjelloun as the receptionist showed me into his office. 'You look awful. Sit down and tell me what illicit pursuits have been keeping you so busy. Pedro was a little vague over the phone. By the way, do you have somewhere to stay while you're here?'

'No. Can you get me a room at that hotel near the port where I stayed last time? I'll only need it for a night, Rachid.'

'So you hope! Can you arrange that for Mr McKinnon please, Farah?' Farah returned after a few minutes with spiced coffee and *ghriba* almond cookies, confirming the booking.

Like most young Moroccan women in this town she was dressed trendily and wore neither a veil nor a headscarf.

'Yes,' Rachid continued. 'Pedro was unclear but he asked me to find out what I could about the *Dalmatia Star*. It wasn't difficult. She sank barely fifteen miles off the coast from here just four days ago. All the crew are safe. In fact, they are in remarkably good shape. I interviewed the master – or acting master I should say – a Captain Mornaric. He's been detained along with the rest of the crew by the port police pending their enquiries into the incident.' He looked across his desk at me with one eyebrow raised.

'Can you get me in to see him, Rachid?'

'I believe so. I am sure you can guess what is suspected.'

'I know. The sea was calm, the sun was shining and the ship was scuttled, but not before the crew had packed their bags, the cook had prepared sandwiches, they'd boarded the lifeboat in an orderly fashion and headed for port.'

'Yes, that is exactly what is suspected. But Captain Mornaric is not admitting it. All he has said is that he would like to meet with you.'

Rachid accompanied me to the Surete Nationale's port police headquarters in the Ain Sebaa arrondissement where the *Dalamtia Star*'s crew were accommodated in several cells shared between them. The police officer-in-charge led us down a corridor to a cell where Mornaric was sitting on a bench in splendid isolation. He looked lost and miserable but brightened up a bit when he saw us. The officer un-locked the cell and led the way up a flight of stairs to a room with a long table and chairs either side.

Having recently been incarcerated myself I sympa-thised with Mornaric's plight, although the facilities here were rather more salubrious than in Kazunda. 'Are you be-ing well treated?' I asked him.

'Yes, but can you get us out of here?'

'You know what they suspect: that you and your ship-mates deliberately scuttled the ship. If so, that can lead to a whole raft of charges.'

'Can I speak with you alone?'

I looked at the police captain. He shrugged. I sensed he wasn't too concerned about the fate of the crew either way. 'Twenty minutes,' he said. Rachid left the room with the officer and I turned back to Mornaric.

'Okay, Juraj, tell me what happened. And relax will you?'

'It was Horvat. He threatened our families. He said if we didn't sink the ship they would be harmed, killed even.'

'Why don't we take it from the beginning?' He was clearly stressed, breathing so heavily I thought he might hy-perventilate. 'Tell me what happened from the time I left the ship off the Portuguese coast. You've only got twenty minutes, remember.'

It turned out that once we had gone ashore with Babic's body, Horvat had taken control with his threat of reprisals against the crew's families. He'd ordered Mornaric to sail the ship south to Tangier. They'd hove to off the port there and after nightfall two RIBs had come alongside. There were ten men in each RIB. They had boarded and the boats had been loaded using ship's gear and lashed to the hatch covers. Horvat had directed the operation and the ship had then continued her voyage south.

The men who had boarded were all from the same place: Novorossiysk, the Russian port on the north-east coast of the Black Sea. It was clear that they knew Horvat and deferred to him. Horvat ordered the crew and officers to double up in each others' cabins and the mercenaries took over the crew's quarters. They were hard, hostile men. Sometimes fights broke out amongst themselves and every day they would exercise and train with the weapons that were already on the ship. Always they were under Horvat's command. Each morning at 0800 Horvat would communicate by satellite phone from the ship's monkey bridge out of earshot. But one morning the second mate had overheard him talking in Russian. Then, on another occasion, Mornaric had been out on the bridge wing and had heard Horvat again up on the monkey bridge but this time speaking in English. It was a long conversation and at one point he was talking to someone about flights from Zurich to Brazzaville.

'Any idea who he was talking to?

'Knowing what I know now I believe it was

Jawad Mendesa.'

Eight days out of Tangier the ship had reached Kazunda and anchored several miles off the port.

'Did you ever see or hear of a submarine in the area?' I asked him. He had not.

'What about when the attack on the floatel took place?'

'Those missiles came from way out in the Atlantic. Maybe from a submarine, I don't know. It was very frightening to watch.'

'How about the attack on the helicopter?'

'Those were launched from the ship, by the mercenaries. The missile launcher and missiles were all part of the cargo. They secured the launcher on the hatch cover of number one hold.' It was as we had guessed.

All but four of the mercenaries had disembarked with the RIBs. The landing craft were loaded with the APCs and the Warriors, and the convoy had headed for the coast under cover of darkness. Horvat had remained on board the ship.

'And you assisted with all this on Horvat's instructions?'

'We had no choice, believe me. What would you have done in that situation? We lifted everything that was going ashore, the RIBs, landing craft and all the weapons, using ship's gear. We just had to do what we were told.'

'Did any of the mercenaries return to the ship?'

Mornaric gave a bitter laugh. 'No. As soon as Horvat heard what was happening ashore he ordered us to sail north. I'm sure they were all killed in the fighting but anyway he abandoned them.'

'I want to know where and when Mendesa comes into the picture, Juraj.'

'I don't know. I'm guessing, but I believe he met up with the mercenaries when they went ashore. He must have taken over command from Horvat to oversee the assault on the city and the palace. But we never saw him on the ship.'

'And when you arrived off Casablanca what were Horvat's orders?'

'To scuttle the ship. He took the ship's own RIB with the four Russian mercenaries who'd stayed on board and told us to take the lifeboat. We thought he was going to shoot us all. After all, we were witnesses to everything that had happened. I think he would have done that but he knew we would have put up a fight and he didn't want to run the risk of a fight he might lose – even with his four mercenaries. We would not have given in. We had taken a few assault rifles and pistols from the cargo and hidden them in the engine room. Anyway, he was in a hurry to get ashore. He just reminded us what would happen to our families if we didn't sink the ship. He held that threat over our heads.'

'Any idea where Horvat would have gone after he came ashore here?'

'I don't know, but he was very upset with Mendesa. I speak a little Russian. I heard him tell the mercenaries that

Mendesa was the cause of the coup's failure because the presidential guard would not support him and neither would the people. Mendesa had claimed he had the support of the people but that was a lie, he said. I got the feeling he was out to get Mendesa.'

And at that moment the port police officer came back into the room with Rachid and a sergeant. 'Your time is up, Captain,' the officer announced. 'We shall discuss this case with these two gentlemen, meanwhile you and your crew will remain in our custody here.'

'Can you help us?' Mornaric implored me.

'We'll do what we can,' I said, and with that he was escorted back to his cell.

'Captain,' I said to the police officer, 'the *Dalmatia Star* sank in unexplained circumstances off your coast. She was in international waters at the time of the accident and so flag state law and not port state law applies. This is clear.'

Rachid nodded. 'He is right, Captain.'

'So I am formally requesting that you release Captain Mornaric and his crew. Rachid here will arrange accommodation for them pending their repatriation to Croatia. I authorise these expenses on behalf of the ship's owners and her P&I insurers. Rachid, you will receive the authority in writing from the CMM's office in Scotland. Furthermore, in the unlikely event of any pollution from the ship's fuel tanks affecting the Moroccan coastline, any cleaning up and compensation expenses will also be taken care of under the terms of the ship's liability insurance. And if Captain Mornaric is required to attend any local inquiry, then we undertake on the owner's behalf that he will make himself available here in Casablanca and Mr Benjelloun will provide legal counsel. I believe that will take care of this matter and you need have no further concerns.'

'I hear what you say, but as you both must know, an act of barratry has been committed, an act of gross misconduct committed by a master or crew of a vessel, and this includes illegal scuttling.'

Rachid interjected: 'We would argue that in legal terms a crime has not been committed. If the ship was deliberately scuttled, and we do not concede that it was, then the master and his crew would have done so under duress, under threat from a senior employee of the ship's owners. If the owner himself chooses to wreck the ship, no crime is committed as the owner is simply destroying his own property. Mr McKinnon has offered you a convenient solution, a way of avoiding a lengthy criminal trial with an uncertain outcome. I would urge you to take his offer seriously and convey it to your senior officers.'

'Very well. You know the law and I hope you are right,' the officer replied. 'I have no wish to detain them further than is necessary. Provided my superiors agree and we receive these assurances from the insurers in Scotland, then I will authorise their release. '

'Good,' I said. 'Rachid, would you report these discussions to the CMM and ask them for their authority to settle on the terms I've outlined? It should only be a formality.'

We left it like that. Mornaric and his crew had been through a hell of an ordeal. I was reasonably confident they would be released within the next week or two. What I wasn't so sure of was what might happen to them once back in Croatia if Horvat was still storming around.

And I was no closer to finding Mendesa.

CHAPTER 25

'You don't have to do it, Angus. There are others who are paid and trained to clean up this kind of mess.'

'How many times have you told me this in the past?'

'So don't. Your job is done my love. Drop the whole thing and let Six or the Cousins take care of the bastards. I imagine the CIA would be more than happy to send a bunch of Navy SEALS in to avenge the murder of their brothers-in-arms.'

'I have to,' I said. Cold-blooded executions were not in my line of work, but with Mendesa it was different. It was personal.

This was the first chance I'd had to see Claire since I'd left Lisbon for Kazunda and I was relieved to find her in good spirits. She was still in the Hospital da Luz. She'd told me she was making good progress but the doctors wanted to keep her there for observation. That wasn't quite the way I'd heard it from Doctor Sanches when I'd spoken to her on the phone the previous day. I'd told her I wanted a straight answer and not platitudes. Claire was making good progress, she'd confirmed. Mentally, she'd recovered well. There was no brain damage though she remembered nothing of the accident, which was normal. Her leg though would take months to heal completely.

But Claire was having none of that. She'd been assigned a young physiotherapist called Santiago who was drop-dead gorgeous she enthused, and was helping her regain her normal range of motion, strength and functional mobility in the injured leg.

'They're removing the fixed cast next week and I'll get a removable one to replace it.'

She was still using crutches, but to demonstrate her progress she walked up and down the living room which formed part of a private suite they'd given her. And she'd still got the security detail to protect her round the clock.

'I haven't a clue what it's all costing and neither do I care. I just want to get out of here on my own two legs unaided by these things,' she said, waving the crutches around.

Claire had always been fit. She'd run the Edinburgh Marathon twice. Now she talked of doing the toughest foot race on earth, the Marathon des Sables – six marathons in six days, carrying everything you need to survive for the week, in the Sahara Desert.

'I'll do it too,' she said. 'You can look like that Angus, but watch me. I will.'

I didn't want my scepticism to discourage her. She needed goals to focus on.

'So they've briefed you,' I said, bringing the conversation back to the case.

'Yes, they have. And we've made some progress. I'm still your case officer, remember?'

'How could I forget?'

'They want you back in Blighty. There's a meeting in London the day after tomorrow. I'll be participating from here. We've got all the COFDM comms in place for the video link.' I hadn't a clue how Coded Orthogonal Frequency Division Multiplexing worked but I'd been told it was very secure.

I smiled. 'And you were just telling me my job was done. What kind of meeting?' I asked warily.

'Don't go all paranoid, darling. They're not going to give you the third degree. You're the big hero now. They just want you to brief them. It's poor old Grant who's being roasted alive over in Langley.'

'You told me once paranoia was a job skill in this business. Anyway, who's attending?' I was still suspicious.

'It's IMTF – Amber Dove's back by the way, long story – Six and, wait for it, some bloke from the SBS.'

'What's been happening then?'

'Well, while you were in Casablanca playing nursemaid to the *Dalmatia Star*'s crew, others have been busy going after the bad guys.'

'Tell me.'

'Horvat and what remained of his band of merry mercenaries high-tailed it back to Novorossiysk. As we thought, he was GRU: military intelligence, the clumsy idiots who tried to do away with the Skripals in Salisbury. They're being reined in by Putin we understand. Anyway, we've got an international arrest warrant out on Horvat and we're watching him too. I don't think he'll be leaving Russia any time soon.'

'He murdered Luca Babic. He's played a leading role in this whole affair. He needs to be brought to account.'

'Yes, well good luck with that, unless you want to go after him in Russia, which I don't recommend. Do you think Horvat was acting under Mendesa's instructions or vice versa?'

'It depends who you talk to. They'd probably each tell you they were the other's controller. Anyway, it's Mendesa who's the chief *bastardo* in all this.'

'And that's the big news. We have eyes on Mendesa.'

'Where is he?'

'He boarded a ship in Ceuta. You know we've been perfecting a crafty way of locating ships that don't want to be found?'

'And what's that?'

'Well, as you know, they like to switch off their AIS.' The Automatic Identification System tracks ships of over

500 gross tons providing identification, position, course and speed. It's used by other ships, vessel traffic services and, when necessary, by the intelligence services,

particularly the IMTF.

'We just run a satellite search across a set of coordinates which spots all ships in that area, then discount those that do have their AIS on. That leaves those that don't but should have and we work from there. It becomes a process of elimination, then of analysing the suspects. Simple. And now with the new software they've given us it takes less than five minutes to get the result.'

'So where's this ship headed?'

'We don't know. She's still in Ceuta. She was on our list of suspect vessels, that is to say AIS off when it should have been on. She'd already taken on bunkers there. She sailed, then returned to port. So they ran some checks and found she'd been chartered out to a firm that might ring a bell with you.'

'West Africa Development Factoring?'

'Bingo! The sovereign wealth investment arm of the former Kazunda government, which Mendesa had wrested control of. He's not stupid is he.'

'So what's the next step? I could be down in Ceuta tomorrow.' It was only fifty miles east of Tangier, to where there were regular flights from Lisbon.

'Hold your horses, sweetheart. They want to wait and

see where she's headed before they act.'

'But Mendesa is definitely on the ship?'

'Correct.'

'And this is where the SBS comes in, I presume.' The Special Boat Service, the UK's maritime special forces unit, had been under the command of the Royal Navy since 2001, and so was closely affiliated with the IMTF. When needed, they served as the IMTF's armed gang, providing on-tap black-op services anywhere there was the kind of trouble suited to their particular talents.

'Possibly. You'll find out at the meeting, I imagine. Listen, Angus, there's something else you need to know.' She propped her crutches against the wall and sat down beside me on the little sofa. She was very close and her hair brushed against my face. It smelled fresh and her scent was so familiar I was stirred by the intimacy of it. I put my arm round her and we kissed. She was soft and warm. It seemed an age since we'd been together like this. Then she pulled away gently.

'Easy, tiger,' she said in a soft, sultry voice that only made me want her more. I took a deep breath.

'Tell me.'

'You know I'd been to see someone from Banco Imperio before the "accident"?' This was something I'd been meaning to ask her about, but had put to the back of my mind as events overtook us all.

'I'd made a contact there: a junior manager in the bank's business development department. We got on well and she invited me to her house for dinner. I met her husband and children, even her old mother, who lived with them. They stayed in a little place on the coast north of Cabo da Roca. It was just one of those contacts you make on a case: someone you think might have something of interest to tell you. Her name is Maria Da Rosa.'

'What was your cover?'

'I told her I was looking for potential investors for an ailing shipowner client: white knights and all that. True, right? We had wine and a nice dinner. We talked. And she told me something which at the time I dismissed as unimportant. After the hit I forgot everything about that evening. I woke up here and gradually some things began to come back, but nothing about that evening, not the dinner, not the crash.'

'Just as well.'

'Yes, but then, just a couple of days ago, she came to see me. She'd heard what had happened. She'd tracked me down and asked the hospital if she could visit. I cleared it with the security guys and said yes. And then in she walks with a huge bunch of flowers. She said she felt so guilty for not coming to see me earlier but her mother had been ill, et cetera.'

'So what did she say?'

'I told her I had no recollection of anything that had happened that evening and asked her what we'd been discussing. She reminded me that I'd said I was exploring possible rescue options open to Dalmatia Shipping and asked her whether Banco Imperio might be interested in investing. That night she had told me that her boss had been spending a lot of time in Zurich lately but she didn't know what for. She added that she'd mentioned my suggestion to him and he'd said he'd be happy to discuss it with me, if and when I was well enough. She said he was in Zurich now and due back at the weekend.'

'Do you think they had anything to do with the attempt on your life, and mine?'

'It's possible isn't it. But she was genuinely upset when she came to visit me. She didn't have to, did she. And she told me something else. I asked her whether the bank was strong enough to take on a risky investment like Dalmatia Shipping. She said the bank had billions in gold bullion stored in its vaults. I asked her where the vaults were. I was fishing. The vaults are in Porto, she said.'

'We don't know enough about them do we,' I said, 'except that they have a dubious record. Pedro warned me to stay away from them and I met Mariana instead.'

'Why don't you get him to do some discreet probing now? Don't let him get in harm's way though. He's not even on our books.'

'Is anyone on our books? Anyway, it's an idea. The bank needs to be checked out even if only to cross them off the list of suspects. We can't ignore the link that Benny Carasso provided from the letter of credit for the Trabzon arms shipment.'

'That's what I was following up on. That's why she told me about her boss spending so much time in Zurich. But I don't want her in harm's way either.'

'Okay. She may be perfectly harmless, in which case we don't want to compromise her. But she may be involved, in which case she's poison.'

'It's highly unlikely that she's involved in anything nasty. That's my belief.'

'Nevertheless, Claire, I think whoever ran you off the road knew about your dinner appointment with her.'

'So she's being watched, you think? And she came to see me here.'

'I'll talk to Summers about tightening up your security.'

We talked on and when I was leaving I hugged her gently. 'Give me a proper hug,' she said. 'I won't break into tiny pieces.' I pulled her closer to me.

***

That evening I had dinner with Pedro at another of his Fado haunts in Alfama. Now he knew I was a fan he was eager to show me more. I told him of the failed coup, which was already big news in Lisbon. He knew of Loma's execution and Mendesa's failed attempt to seize power. And he knew of Nzinga's accession of course – the news had been full of it. I told him of Mariana's part in it all. And then I told him about Maria Da Rosa, the contact Claire had made at Banco Imperio before she'd been hit.

'Pedro, you told me weeks ago to stay away from the bank but they are part of this whole business, I'm sure of it. I need to find out what their agenda is, their hidden agenda I mean. They're playing a bigger part in this game than we've realised.' And I told him about the Banco Imperio's gold deposits being stored in Porto.

He gave a low whistle and then nodded thoughtfully. 'Actually, it makes sense. There were good gold smelting facilities in Porto after the war, and no questions asked. Okay, leave it with me. I'll do some digging. What did Claire say to this woman?'

'She sounded her out as to the bank's interest in taking a stake in Dalmatia Shipping. They need a serious investor to bail them out. The woman said she'd mentioned it to her boss, who'd been travelling to Zurich a lot in recent weeks. But there's no need for you to meet her, Pedro. We don't want her exposed to any risk over this, or you either.'

CHAPTER 26

I'd been to Hartside House before. It was a black site detention centre used by the IMTF and other intelligence agencies to interrogate people who had secrets they were reluctant to disclose. Situated in the Buckinghamshire countryside and surrounded by a hundred acres of woods and parkland, the late eighteenth-century mansion looked like just another of England's many old country piles. Built by an officer of the Honourable East India Company who had made good on the back of the opium trade with China, it had been requisitioned in the Second World War by the War Office and remained in the hands of the state ever since.

I was transported to this place of dubious purposes in an unmarked Jaguar. I sat beside the driver but we didn't talk much. The heater created a cosy fug and as the wipers swept monotonously across the windscreen I felt myself drifting off. It was early December and the trees and hedgerows were bare. Rain slanted across this bleak landscape driven in by a cold north-easterly wind off the Russian

Steppe. I woke up as we slowed down in front of a pair of huge wrought-iron gates. The security check at the lodge house was conducted by a burly man in his late fifties with a bald head and a military moustache. He was accompanied by an unfriendly Alsatian who tried to get at me through the passenger window. When we arrived at the house Amber Dove was standing on the steps at the front door. She was wearing a black quilted overcoat with a fur hood. Amber was noticeably slimmer than when I'd last seen her, and I wondered whether the weight loss was due to stress or diet. Her manner was brusque but friendly.

'Welcome once again, Angus!' she exclaimed, gripping my hand. 'And before you ask, I'm back running the show; at least this case at least. Then off to Tuscany never to be heard of again.'

'You deserve a rest, Amber, but I'm glad you're in on this one. Who else is here?'

'Ben Wood who you'll remember from last time, and a couple of specialists. And Claire of course, on the video link, poor girl. How did you find her? I went down to see her in Lisbon you know, when you were in Kazunda. She was being well looked after.'

'She's good. It'll take time but you know Claire, she's nothing if not resolute.'

'And thank God for that. Come on in and I'll introduce you.'

Four people were standing around in the conference room drinking coffee and talking among themselves.

'Ben Wood you'll remember from the last time,' said Amber, interrupting the group. I still had no idea if Ben Wood was his real name. He'd been assigned from MI6 as an observer on the last IMTF case I'd been involved in, but there had been little doubt in anyone's mind that his real purpose was to uncover weaknesses within the IMTF in preparation for a takeover. And that was what I thought had transpired, with Amber Dove being the scapegoat. Only Amber Dove was back in charge even if only temporarily. Ben had tamed his mountain-man beard into a neat goatee since I'd last seen him, but was still wearing a suit that looked several sizes too small for him.

Amber continued the introductions. 'Now then, Captain Bob Fraser commands HMS *Buttress*. I suspect you'll be seeing quite a bit of each other from now on and I'll let Bob tell you all about his wonderful ship in due course.

'And Lieutenant Commander George Conway here is in command of the SBS's C Squadron. I thought it would be useful to get his take on all these goings-on, and again, we'll be in need of his services before long. Likewise with Lieutenant Kate Henderson here. Kate is from 18 UKSF Signal Regiment. She is also acting as liaison officer on this case between the intelligence services, including GCHQ, and the military.'

They were both in civilian clothing. Kate Henderson was a serious young woman who I'd encountered once before. She'd told me she lived in Herefordshire close to the Special Forces home base at Stirling Lines where her own regiment also operated from, but spent a lot of time in Cheltenham with GCHQ, which was only forty miles away.

George Conway, who I hadn't met before, was a cheerful individual with an intelligent face and hair long enough to give a warrant officer apoplexy. I estimated he was over six and a half foot tall.

By contrast Bob Fraser, an equally amiable Scot, was short and broad with a bald head that shone under the light.

We all shook hands. I poured myself a coffee and we sat down round the table facing the top of the room where three large screens were positioned. As we were settling down one of the screens came alive and there was Claire sitting in her hospital room. She waved one of her crutches and we all clapped.

'So, to business,' said Amber Dove. 'Angus, I believe Claire has told you that we now have eyes on Mendesa. He boarded a ship in the Spanish enclave of Ceuta on the Mediterranean side of the Moroccan coast. The ship replenished bunkers there and Mendesa took delivery of her onto timecharter on behalf of this West Africa Development Factoring outfit you'd uncovered. The agent has confirmed all of this. For Immigration clearance purposes, Jawad Mendesa was signed on the crew articles as a supernumerary, so he wasn't being particularly careful.

'The ship passed through the Straits of Gibraltar about six hours ago and is headed north, destination unknown.' She activated one of the screens with a remote control and a picture of a roll-on roll-off ship appeared. 'This is the vessel, a ro-ro: the *Poseidon Pioneer*. Her AIS is off of course, but we're tracking her by our own eye in the sky.'

'Any cargo on board?' I asked.

'No cargo was declared when she entered and cleared Ceuta but that doesn't mean a lot. We're still waiting for Lloyd's to give us her previous ports of call and cargo particulars. They've promised to have an answer for us by 1400 today Kate says, so within the next hour or so.

'This ship seems to have popped up out of nowhere; probably re-registered and renamed prior to her arrival in Ceuta.'

'Just a note here,' interrupted Bob Fraser. 'Ro-ro ships have large external doors close to the waterline and open vehicle decks with few internal bulkheads, making it a high-risk design which had led to several well-publicised casualties. If the loading door-cum-ramp isn't properly closed, once at sea the ship can take on water, which will slop around the vehicle deck and set up a free surface effect making the ship unstable and prone to capsizing. Sorry, that's all.'

'Thanks, Bob. For now though,' Amber continued, 'I

want everyone to be aware of what we know so far. So Angus, would you like to pull it all together for us?'

Amber sat down as I stood and moved to the top of the room. I'd submitted a full report to both Amber and Claire the previous evening. Now I ran through it, covering pretty much everything from Claire's original investigation into Dalmatia Shipping, to Babic's suicide, or murder, the attempts on our own lives, and the events in Kazunda leading to Nzinga's investiture as president. I covered Grant's role as senior case officer but made no mention of anyone's culpability or of Grant's equivocal position vis-á-vis the IMTF, MI6 and CIA which, in my view, clearly had a direct bearing on this case. That was a question for Amber if anyone asked. I just spelled out the events as they'd occurred, including Claire's account of her meetings with Maria da Rosa.

I went into the assistance provided by Benny Carasso and Gudrun Sandmeier in uncovering the link between Mendesa's WADF sovereign wealth fund, Credit Sud of Zurich and Banco Imperio, and the transfer of gold from Germany via Switzerland to the Portuguese bank during and after the war, firstly in payment for the purchase of tungsten exports to Nazi Germany and secondly, after the war, to fund ODESSA.

And although I'd never met Jawad Mendesa, I recounted what I'd heard from Cordeiro and others regarding his psychopathic behaviour and his alleged responsibility for war crimes, including rape and murder, committed against Kazundan citizens.

I detailed Horvat's role as a GRU agent and the ambiguity over whether he was directing Mendesa, or vice versa, commenting that I felt the most likely explanation was that Mendesa was Russia's useful idiot, or at least their stalking horse as Cordeiro had maintained, and Horvat was there to manage the operation. That had been the plan, but neither of them had acted according to that plan. By any measure it had been a botched operation. Horvat was typical of the ham-fisted kind of GRU agent we had seen much of in recent times, and Mendesa was a clever but dangerous maniac. It was not a match made in heaven but nonetheless the Russians were behind it, although Mendesa had his own agenda. In part it was a case of mutual interests being upset by clashing personalities, and the overall incompetence of those directing it from the GRU's headquarters in Moscow.

'But make no mistake,' I said, 'the big play was by the Russians, in fulfilment of their strategic aims in Africa, which were unsuccessfully countered by our Cousins in Langley.'

I speculated that the missile attack on the *Sea-En Resolution* came from a Russian submarine out in the Atlantic, and asked whether this had been verified. It had. And I described Cordeiro's role, his political leanings and his murder by parties unknown, pointing out that both the CIA and the GRU had cause for grievance against him.

Finally, I went back to Claire's finding that gold bullion held by Banco Imperio was apparently stored in vaults in the port city of Porto.

'Banco Imperio's role in this case has not been fully exposed or understood yet,' I concluded, 'but it is said that Portugal is still sitting on most of the gold it received in payment for its tungsten sales to Nazi Germany. Some say there's still four hundred tons of it stashed away both in Portugal and elsewhere. My best guess is that Banco Imperio is offshoring its share well away from the prying eyes of those who wish to see it surrendered and returned to whoever the Nazis looted it from. It's a divisive issue in Portugal today but Antonio Salazar always maintained the gold was legitimate payment for the tungsten sales. Squirrelled away somewhere in Africa where it can be used to acquire arms and materiel, for bribing corrupt politicians or funding coups, would make sense. The bank's business plan is focused on investment in Portugal's former African colonies, legitimately or otherwise. And it's also my guess that they're playing footsie with the Kremlin along the way.'

I'd drawn a rough diagram. It remained for them to join the dots. And as if on cue, Kate Henderson received a signal on her phone, got up and left the room returning a few minutes later. 'Lloyd's say the ship loaded trucks and other equipment in the Black Sea port of Trabzon.'

'Where the *Dalmatia Star* loaded,' said Amber. 'I don't

suppose they knew her final destination? Do we know her latest position?'

'Passing Lisbon now, still heading north.'

And you didn't need to be a psychic to know where the *Poseidon Pioneer* was headed.

There followed hours of discussion during which everyone had their say. We sketched out differing scenarios and argued the details of the operation inside out. Only Claire left the meeting. She had suddenly looked worn out.

The meeting turned into an informal war games exercise in which we projected every possible eventuality given what scant information we had as to the *Poseidon Pioneer*'s future movements. We could be reasonably certain that the ship, with Mendesa on board, was heading for Porto, presumably to load some or all of Banco Imperio's gold bullion. What then? It was unlikely the ship would continue northbound or westward across the Atlantic so we focused our attention on her southbound options – either eastward back into the Med or south down the African coast. But to where?

CHAPTER 27

'So,' Amber announced, addressing George Conway and myself after the others had left. 'There'll be a navy Puma arriving to pick the two of you up from here at 0700 tomorrow. It will drop you aboard the *Buttress* as she's leaving Devonport. Thereafter you'll be kept informed of developments as we receive further intel ourselves. Don't underestimate the opposition. Just because they failed last time doesn't mean they will again. And remember, the GRU are behind this. Covertly perhaps: they can't afford to have their involvement broadcast. But rest assured we will know more of their intentions than they know of ours, and to maintain that position the element of surprise is crucial.'

Conway and I stayed at Hartside that night. After dinner we had a couple of drinks in the bar and turned in early. We'd talked of many things, but not the operation that lay ahead. We were getting the measure of each other I guess.

The Puma landed on the lawn outside the house where a large H set in a circle had been marked out in yellow to guide it in. The rain had turned to sleet overnight and the wind had strengthened. I'd developed an aversion to helicopters since the ditching episode off Kazunda. The Puma was more substantial than the little Robinson we'd gone down in, but that didn't make me feel any more confident.

We took off into the buffeting wind, skimming the tall chimneypots of the old house and heading west. It took us just under two hours' flying time at an altitude of twelve hundred feet and against the strong headwind before we began our descent onto the flight deck of HMS *Buttress* as she was sailing past the breakwaters on her way out of Plymouth Sound. The Puma landed with a thump and as I slowly released my vice-like grip on the armrests, Conway looked across the aisle and treated me to a relaxed smile. He knew of the ditching accident. The flight deck crew beckoned us over to the control island, where I was greeted by the officer of the day who introduced himself as Lieutenant Gordon Jenkins. 'This ship's our very own Swiss Army knife,' he announced in a confident Welsh accent as we made our way forward to the captain's quarters. 'Does anything and everything.'

Captain Bob Fraser had returned the previous night. 'Welcome aboard,' he said as we entered his dayroom. 'Coffee?' He waved us over to two armchairs and sat down opposite us.

After the steward had brought in the coffee another

officer entered the room. 'Ah,' said Fraser getting up. 'Commander Geoff Williams. Geoff is equivalent to your Chief Officer, Angus. Thought it would be useful for the four of us to have a chat about the operation.

'First I'll give you a quick rundown on the ship. We're a landing platform dock, or LPD. Our role is to support the Royal Marines, the SBS included of course, ashore, by air and by sea - and in a big way. We've got boats in the landing dock in the belly of the ship. We've got assault helicopters on the flight deck. We can carry 256 troops with their vehicles and combat supplies – up to 405 troops when necessary. George here will show you those parts of the ship relevant to the mission. Anything you need to know, just ask.'

We spent the next hour running through the role HMS *Buttress* would play as we sailed south tracking the *Poseidon Pioneer*. Then the steward was summoned back to show us to our cabins, each comprising a single bed, metal wardrobe and cupboard, and a washbasin. The showers and heads were down the passageway.

Yet another lieutenant took me down to the dock, which was the part of the ship that interested me the most. And it was here that Conway's sixteen-man troop was introduced one by one. They were all burly men, all bearded and dressed in jeans and T-shirts despite the near freezing temperature.

Occupying the dock was an array of vehicles and equipment, including four landing craft, or LCUs. 'Very similar to what were used for the D-Day landings,' explained Conway, 'except the wheelhouse is on the starboard side nowadays so we drive on through the stern door and off through the bow. *Buttress'* primary role is to transfer personnel, vehicles and equipment onto hostile shores - perfect for our little job. Flat-bottomed of course, so bloody uncomfortable at sea. No bow or stern thrusters – they make too much noise: a sub could hear them miles away.'

Loaded into each of the LCUs were four Jackals. Conway reeled off their virtues: 'Emwimmiks we call them: Mobility Weapon-Mounted Installation Kits if you want to know what it stands for. Primary role is deep battlespace reconnaissance, rapid assault and fire support – roles where mobility, endurance and manoeuvrability are important. They're agile and well-armed. These are what we'll be using when we get wherever we're going – all four of them. Five men per vehicle and as well as your good self we'll bring along a few other specialists, so twenty of us in all.'

We went up on deck to where four LCVP Mk5s were suspended from davits. Lieutenant Dave Stephenson, a cheerful Geordie from the Special Reconnaissance Regiment, recited their purpose: 'Landing Craft Vehicle Personnel. Primary role, putting men and equipment ashore. But we also use them as patrol boats. Can carry up to thirty-five fully-laden Marines and their equipment including Land

Rovers.' Stephenson's special forces regiment was part of the British Army but I'd been told they worked closely with the SBS as well as the SAS.

We met that evening in a bar next to the wardroom: Fraser, who was there by invitation according to some unfathomable Navy protocol, Conway, Stephenson, our host Williams and myself. The ship's officers were dressed in Red Sea rig: uniform trousers, open-neck tropical white shirt with boards and maroon cummerbund with the ship's crest. On the advice of the captain I had borrowed a cummerbund to conform to this protocol. Fraser recommended Horse's Necks meticulously prepared by the bar steward. Dinner with the other ship's officers followed in the wardroom. It was all in striking contrast to life on a merchant vessel.

By the following day we were crossing the Bay of Biscay which, in December, was as rough as its reputation. As commanding officer the captain was on the bridge frequently. The officer of the watch, navigating officer, lookout and quartermaster on the wheel were all there too, lending a mood of busy camaraderie though there was little idle chatter.

But most of that day and those that followed were spent with Conway and his troop down in the dock or on shooting practice from the flight deck. Given the weather conditions, this was challenging. The targets were cardboard boxes and I was given a Colt Canada C8 assault rifle and a Sig P226 pistol to play with. For the rest of the voyage I practised for at least three hours daily. By the time we were ready to disembark I was getting the hang of it, and of the infrared night vision goggles.

'Night vision illuminates the surrounding darkness while thermal imaging illuminates darkened targets,' Conway explained. 'While the optic itself is mounted on your rifle, what it sees is beamed via a Bluetooth connection to your head-mounted display so you can toggle between the two modes at the push of a button. Simple.'

Throughout the voyage the ops room status was continuously at "ready for action" level. The ship was fully armed with missile systems ready for launch. And on day three we received confirmation that the *Poseidon Pioneer* had made her call at Porto and was sailing south. This information had come from Pedro, who had reported direct to Claire in Lisbon, and it had been cross-checked against a similar report from the Lloyd's Agent in Porto. What Pedro had also discovered, and was not in the Lloyd's report, was that three large trucks had driven off the vessel and proceeded to a location on the south bank of the Rio Douro several miles upstream from the city. They'd returned after eight hours and the ship had sailed. This put her around six hundred nautical miles ahead of our own present position on the *Buttress*.

What was more, again from Pedro's discreet enquiries, was the ship's destination: the port of Nouadhibou in Mauritania. My case work had never taken me to this port but it was well known in shipping circles, for Nouadhibou was the biggest ships graveyard in the world. Vessels of all flags, mostly flags of convenience, big and small and from nations across the world were dumped here having outlived their usefulness or because the owners, for whatever reason, had wanted to steer clear of the international law of the sea.

Now we knew our quarry's destination, *Buttress* picked up speed to close the gap between the two ships. 'Now the chase begins,' Conway announced. 'We can put some meat on the bones of those war games we've been playing.' And after further reports channelled through Amber Dove, came in over the next couple of days, Conway was able to give Fraser, Williams, Stephenson and myself a briefing on how he saw the landside operation playing out.

We gathered in Fraser's dayroom but this was Conway's show now. The atmosphere had changed: there was a palpable sense of urgency and anticipation of what lay ahead. 'Okay, I'll keep this brief,' he began. 'First off, we can assume the *Poseidon Pioneer* is carrying gold in those three trucks, and we're pretty sure that this op is going to be moving inland once the ship reaches Nouadhibou. So from here on in we'll be sharing operational control with the Special Forces unit at RAF Akrotiri. There are several good reasons for this which I won't go into now. Suffice it to say that Mauritania is manageable from Cyprus. Not that close but they have all the aircraft, men, equipment and logistics to support a long-range job like this and they're used to operating in the desert: Iraq, Syria, Afghanistan – these countries are Akrotiri's backyard.

'Buttress will be able to provide whatever further support we may need but will reduce speed and continue southwards serving as a decoy against any interest from foreign parties out there in the Atlantic, such as our Russian friends. Both the Americans and our own navy have assets able to deflect any hostile action from that direction. However, I would stress this is primarily a criminal and not a military target we're pursuing. And if all goes well, we would hope to wrap it up within thirty-six hours; but we have contingency planning in place for much longer if necessary.

'So first we locate the *Poseidon Pioneer* in Nouadhibou. That's Stephenson's job with his LCVPs. If the gold is on board the ship then we'll mount an assault there and then, but we're all pretty certain our eyes in the sky will tell us that it's not. Our guess: it'll be heading ashore in those trucks. Right so far, Angus?'

I nodded. We'd discussed it at length down in the dock. Now Conway continued.

'In the air we'll have an assortment of aircraft from Akrotiri including an E3D Sentry providing airborne early warning and control – AWAKS in other words; a Reaper UAV feeding real-time images back to Akrotiri with a downlink to me on the ground; and, crucially, two Hercules C130s – and you know what they're for. They'll only be called in once we're ready. It's a long way from Akrotiri and then on to Lisbon so we'll have a Voyager air-to-air refuelling tanker in the air too.

'Finally, you don't need to be reminded that this is a black op: covert and fully deniable; under the radar.'

CHAPTER 28

The forty-mile-long peninsula that is Ras Nouadhibou runs down Africa's Atlantic coastline parallel to the mainland. On a map it looks a bit like Baja California on the US west coast, but there the similarity ends, for this is the harsh, remote coast of the Sahara desert. The peninsula is split down the middle between the nations of Mauritania on the east and Western Sahara on the west. It's also known as Cabo Blanco or Cap Blanc, depending on whose map you're looking at.

We arrived off the peninsula at 0200 hours. The sea was calm, the temperature in the mid-twenties. There was no moon and the night was awash with stars, the Milky Way a swathe of pale light painted diagonally across the sky.

Despite reservations from Conway I'd decided to join the team from the Special Reconnaissance Regiment and at 0230 our LCVP was launched from its davits. On board was a six-man team led by Dave Stephenson. Our equipment included two Land Rovers. We set off around the cape in the little craft and headed up the gulf on the peninsula's eastern side north of the port of Nouadhibou. Here was the grave-yard. Spread out in the waters off the port lay over three hundred ships. Some were afloat, others aground on sandbanks and on the beach. They would never be removed. Mauritania was rich in iron ore and had no use for scrap metal. Anyway, the cost of removing the oil and other hazardous liquids from their tanks would far outweigh their value as scrap. We moved in amongst them, our progress made easier by our shallow draft. It was somewhere here that the *Poseidon Pioneer* was anchored.

With guidance from our eye in the sky we found her and hove to some fifty yards away. The ship had been run aground on a sandbank close to the beach. Her bow door was open. She was showing no lights and there was no sign of human activity on the deck: a dead ship. We approached to get a closer look then cautiously began circling her. When we came back round to the bow door I raised my arm for Stephenson to bring us to a stop. Pulling down my infrared goggles I peered into the mouth of the vessel. Now I could see clearly into the garage. It was empty.

'I need to get on board,' I said. 'Can you back onto the bow ramp and give me fifteen minutes?'

'Only if you agree to take a couple of guys with you.'

'Sure,' I agreed. It would speed up the search.

Leaving from the vehicle deck, we carried out a search of the whole ship from the depths of the engine room to the monkey bridge, from stem to stern. It was cursory but I was pretty sure there was no one left on board. If there had been they'd have either come out at us or surrendered: we were armed to the teeth. But time wasn't on our side. The *Poseidon Pioneer*'s cargo of trucks loaded with Nazi gold was gone. The ship had been abandoned to rust away like all the others in that strange, ghostly place.

We rejoined the LCVP. Stephenson reported back to Conway on *Buttress* and got the go-ahead to land on the western side of the gulf and rendezvous with the SBS team at agreed coordinates. We headed out eastwards across the gulf. It was a distance of sixteen nautical miles and took us an hour and fifteen minutes maintaining half-speed so as not to alert any curious fishing boats.

As we hit the beach on the other side we disturbed flocks of birds here on their breeding grounds. Thousands of flamingos, sandpipers, pelicans, terns and other species wintering on this east Atlantic flyway rose into the air. There were four of us including Stephenson and myself. We came ashore in one of the Land Rovers, leaving the remainder of the team on board to await Stephenson's return.

Now we headed south to the rendezvous point just north of the Banc d'Arguin National Park. Here the mud-flats border the desert and the jeep made heavy going of the terrain until we reached harder, drier land. We drove on as dawn broke across the vast, empty expanse of the Sahara.

And after an hour or so we came across Conway's SBS team in their Jackals.

'You found the ship alright then.' We'd already radioed him.

'Yeah, but nothing on board. No trucks, no crew. Nothing,' I said.

'Right,' said Conway. 'Let's get after them.'

Stephenson and his two colleagues headed back to re-join their comrades on the LCVP before returning to *Buttress*. Our aim now was to intercept the three trucks that had come ashore some hours ahead of us. They had landed on the peninsula so would have had to drive north on the N2, a surfaced road that went up to the head of the gulf before heading east then south in a loop. We reckoned the trucks would turn off this road at some point on its southward leg and head further east, deep into the interior of the Sahara. This was based on intel reporting the location of an old French Foreign Legion fort around which the RAF's Reaper UAV had spotted a group of Bedouins with their camels who had just set up a camp there and were carrying arms. The fort had been abandoned for years so this sudden activity made it a site of interest. We would head for it and the Reaper, flying high above the desert, would feed images directly back to Conway in the Jackal. I sat up alongside him and we set off.

The eight-ton Jackal is an ungainly looking vehicle inside and out, painted in camouflage colours and carrying grenade launchers and a heavy machine gun bolted onto a gun turret. It was protected by steel armour plating against mine and ballistic attack. Conway had given me a sermon on its merits as he had on all the rest of his kit: 'Designed to fill a gap between the Land Rover and the slower tanks and heavy vehicles. We wanted something that could carry men, provisions and weapons over rough terrain, quickly: top speed eighty mph. Had to be well protected and well armed of course. And importantly for us, it has a range of five-hundred miles.'

They came with closed cabs or open – ours were open. I was told, and soon it was confirmed, that the suspension was a work of genius. At upwards of half a million sterling each, it needed to be pretty capable.

We headed east into the white glare of the sun as it rose higher from the horizon. Despite the terrain the Jackal glided smoothly along on its magic suspension. We passed no humans or other motor vehicles, only the odd group of moth-eaten camels scratching around in the sand for sprigs of thorn bush. The contrast between this desolate but striking landscape and the lush, decaying jungle of Kazunda was acute.

After an hour we crossed the north–south N2 road, again seeing no traffic, and continued east. This was bandit country. Al Qaeda in the Islamic Maghreb and other terrorist groups were known to operate here. After another hour we'd covered a further fifty miles and Conway stopped, the other three vehicles pulling up alongside us. The cool of the desert night had long since dissipated and now we were stationary, without the breeze from our headway, the heat struck like a blast furnace. We gathered around Conway who, reassuringly, was using a map and compass in addition to his GPS unit and the downlink device hooking us up to the Reaper out of sight in the sky above us. He pointed his finger at a spot on the map. 'We're here, forty-six miles east of the N2.' He pointed to another spot. 'The Reaper's telling us the gold trucks are here. It's identified them as three 6 by 6 Mercedes Zetros off-roaders, each with a ten-ton payload capacity. They're travelling at around our speed – forty to fifty miles an hour. That's faster than we expected. Projecting their direction of travel we reckon they're headed for this point here.' Again he pointed, this time to a symbol, a small tower. 'This is the abandoned French Foreign Legion fort, one of the last Saharan forts built to control tribal unrest in the area back in the 1930s. Rectangular layout with two towers, one in the north-west corner and another in the south-east. And a blockhouse. It also played a key role in the ethnic conflicts that occurred here in the seventies and eighties. There are still potentially hostile tribesmen in the region, mostly from the Regueibat tribe – normally friendly and hospitable, not always though and it's probably them that the Reaper spotted setting up camp there. Oh, and there's the remains of an airstrip. Hasn't been used since the eighties but I don't think that'll be a problem. The Hercs are used to these sorts of condition.'

The irony linking the two forts struck me: this remote, abandoned spot in the desert where I was heading and Black Reef where I'd come from, both failed bastions of colonial rule.

It was clear from where he'd indicated on the map that the trucks were ahead of us but not by far. 'That's not necessarily a bad thing,' he said. 'I reckon we'll reach the fort no more than an hour after them. It'll be well after dark by then. We've still got another eight hours of driving.'

We set off again. The sun was high in the sky now and the light blinding, even with the windproof desert sunglasses we'd been issued. There was no horizon. The sky was the same hazy white as the sand. Mirage lakes would appear then disappear moments before we reached them.

We were travelling faster now. Conway wanted to time our arrival at the fort after the Zetros had arrived but before they'd unloaded the gold and left. It was our best guess that the trucks would have to be carrying forklifts and that the gold would be stowed on pallets. Assuming a load capacity of around eighteen hundred kilograms each and, that according to best-guess intelligence reports we'd received, the *Poseidon Pioneer* had loaded between twenty-two and twenty-five tons of gold, then there would be between twelve and fifteen pallets to shift. Although we could only guess at the distance the forklifts would have to travel from truck to blockhouse, if that's where they were planning to store the hoard, it wasn't going to take long – maybe as little as two or three hours to have the gold safely stored with whatever security systems they were planning to set up there.

Conway was saying: 'Could be this gang of tribesmen or the national military, but I bet they'll have some permanent human presence there to guard something of this value. And I'd be surprised if they don't rig up some kind of booby trap too. What do you reckon that lot's worth?'

'Well over a billion dollars,' I said, 'maybe a billion and a half.'

He whistled. As we pushed on we continued going over the job and how it was likely to unfold once we reached the fort. What we hadn't planned for was the sandstorm.

It was late afternoon when the sky began to darken prematurely. The sun was well behind us now, a dull red orb in the west. With little warning, five or six miles ahead appeared a billowing brown cloud, a swirling mass of sand towering hundreds of feet into the sky. It stretched far across the desert and lay directly in our path like a vertical sandstone cliff. As we got closer we changed from sunglasses to goggles and pulled our Shemagh scarfs up over mouth and nose.

'These storms can travel at twenty-five miles an hour and we're doing fifty so keep your hair on!' shouted Conway. The other three Jackals spread out and switched on their lights. Then we were in it.

At first it was a disorientating churn of brown, but then as the storm closed around us it went completely dark. We slowed down and with headlights on beam, crawled forward.

'How long's this likely to last?' I called.

'Who knows? They've been known to last days, or it could be a couple of hours. The Zetros will have been caught in it too, no doubt.'

The storm brought with it a discordant hissing, howling wind. Sand was everywhere now and got past our protective clothing, into mouth, throat, ears and nose though thankfully not into my eyes, protected by the goggles.

We travelled on, the headlights from the other three Jackals only faintly visible alongside us. At one point we passed three camels plodding along in the gloom. These conditions were nothing out of the ordinary for them. 'No sign of the three wise men!' shouted Conway.

No wise men and no crystal ball. Maybe I could have blamed these Special Forces guys for not thinking outside the box, of taking a rigidly tactical approach, of even thinking that because this was an operation against criminals it was somehow going to be a walk in the park. I could have blamed them for any of these things and blamed myself too, but the truth was that none of us could have anticipated what would happen that night.

"No battle plan survives contact with the enemy," wrote Helmuth von Moltke.

CHAPTER 29

It was another three hours of laborious progress through that storm before anything happened. We were getting close to the fort and Conway slowed us further, down to a crawl.

'Look, there!' I shouted, pointing off to our left: red lights barely visible but uncomfortably close.

'Shit!' Conway yelled back and veered off to the right only pulling up when we were well clear. The other three Jackals followed. We climbed down and met with the rest of the squad seeking what shelter we could behind Conway's vehicle.

Conway had been getting an intermittent flow of intel reports and now was hearing that Mendesa was believed to have assembled a ragtag band of ex-Polisario militia to serve as his mercenary force. Maybe the guys from Novorossiysk had politely excused themselves after what had happened to their comrades. Or more likely Mendesa knew that for the purpose of a showdown in the Sahara desert, the Polisario were better suited. These were men who had abandoned their armed struggle for Sahrawi self-determination in favour of a well-paid mercenary lifestyle. And they were the same group that the Reaper had spotted earlier. What we didn't know was what weaponry they would be carrying and so it had been decided that any attempt to persuade them into surrendering would be an unnecessary and avoidable risk. Conway, who was a veteran of Iraq, Afghanistan and the campaign against IS, had warned me there would be no question of taking prisoners.

'This is it guys. Check your kit. Goggles synced.' he told us all. I checked mine though I was still having difficulty getting to grips with the sense of detached virtual reality they produced. We checked our body armour too, then moved forward on foot. As we got closer I could make out the three big Zetros trucks, now pulled up against the west wall of the fort. All three trucks had their tailgates down and as we approached a forklift truck with a pallet on board, its load covered in plastic sheeting, laboured up a slope and into the fort, its headlights piercing the sand-filled darkness.

Our own group under Conway's command was positioning itself here, twenty yards from the trucks and on the west side of the fort. The other three groups, on Conway's instruction, were entering the fort itself from north, east and south. Peering through a gap in the wall of the old citadel I could make out the fort's blockhouse, a solid-looking three-storey structure on the south side towering above the rest of the ruins.

The firefight that ensued was quick, ruthless and one-sided. Without asking questions, Conway's unit took out all the truck and forklift drivers and the four or five Polisario who'd supposedly been defending them. I counted twelve men lying around the trucks and forklifts, dark patches of blood spreading out into the sand around them. I hadn't fired a shot. The other three units moved in over the ruined walls on the other sides of the fort progressing towards the blockhouse with the same deadly efficiency. Against the Marines' C8 rifles chattering on full auto, their superior night-vision technology and their tight discipline and signalling procedures, the Polisario were no match. Two of Conway's units were left to patrol the whole site and mop up any stray resistance that hadn't already been dealt with. That left ten men including myself encircling the blockhouse.

A silence had descended. Only the moaning of the wind disturbed it. There were men in the blockhouse but before an assault could begin three figures appeared at the entrance, two men and a woman.

I recognised Jawad Mendesa. I'd pored over photographs of this man. He'd been described to me at length. And I'd imagined confronting him, of what I would say to him, and how he would react. Now that time had come. But it was not Mendesa's distinct, hulking form that held my attention but the two figures in front of him. Mariana looked frightened and Grant was trying hard not to.

Mendesa pushed them both forward, prodding them with the barrel of his gun. Both Grant and Mariana had their hands restrained behind their backs. Mariana stumbled and fell. She struggled to her feet awkwardly.

Conway turned to me. 'What the fuck?'

I didn't reply. In moments of extreme danger, time and space seem to freeze. I saw it all but my mind wouldn't process it. I'd abandoned my infrared goggles and could see the three of them in reality now. And they could see me.

Mendesa was wearing a *haik*, the large cloth wrapped around the body which was favoured by Berber tribesmen, and a cloth turban. Grant was wearing the same safari suit he'd worn in Kazunda, only now it was stained with blood. I couldn't see where it had come from. Mariana, despite the fall, now stood frightened but defiant beside Grant. She was wearing jeans and a short blue denim jacket. Her dark hair was tousled and unkempt.

'You look surprised, McKinnon,' Mendesa said. 'Have you come all this way for the gold or to rescue your friends? You will have neither. Tell your toy soldiers here to leave, or if they prefer, stay and watch what I do with these two, and then to you.'

To make the point he tugged hard on Mariana's hair, jerking her head back violently. She screamed.

If I didn't do something fast, Conway would and I

didn't trust that his "take no prisoners" line of thinking would not include those who got in the way.

Without giving it much thought, I threw my rifle to the ground and raised my arms. 'I have a proposition, Mendesa. Let these two go and take the gold. You can't have offloaded much. Take it in your trucks wherever you like.'

'You really expect me to trust you? No. I will take the woman. I have things I look forward to doing with her. As for this CIA scum?' he said, and thrust Grant forward. Then he grabbed Mariana round the neck and, holding her in front of him, raised his gun and fired. It was a machine pistol I recognised: a Glock 19. Of the fifteen rounds in its magazine Mendesa fired the lot on auto. They tore into Grant and punched him forward, his back arching as he let out a short cry before hitting the ground. He didn't move after that. Grant Douglas was dead.

Mariana screamed again and tried to break free. Simultaneously one of Conway's men from the unit that had come from the south side of the fort appeared round the edge of the blockhouse and aimed his rifle at Mendesa. Mendesa caught sight of him and backed through the blockhouse entrance, dragging Mariana with him. As they disappeared into the blackness I drew the Sig and went in after them.

Conway shouted, 'McKinnon! Come back for God's sake, you bloody fool.'

I didn't reply. The images of Grant lying there still and

silent, face down in the sand, of Mariana's face as she was dragged back inside, and of Mendesa, were simultaneously replaying in my head. At that moment I knew clearly the foolhardiness of what I was doing. I just didn't care. A kind of madness had gripped me and when I tried to rationalise it later, it occurred to me that my subconscious was reacting with madness to counter the threat of a madman. In such heat-of-battle moments, how many countless others had reacted with such irrational instinct, and perished as a result?

Conway's men were better equipped, better trained, better able to deal with the situation but I could tell from the sporadic bursts of gunfire that they hadn't finished wiping out the Polisarios. I'd never given them the chance to intervene before I'd reacted. Mendesa was mine. My fury defied reason. I only thought of what the man had done: of everyone he'd abused, tortured and killed. Of what he'd do to Nzinga and the citizens of Kazunda if he got the chance. And more immediately what he'd just down to Grant and would do to Mariana. But despite this flood of jumbled reflexes, one part of my brain remained cold and clear.

The blockhouse was built out of local rock and adobe bricks. The walls were several feet thick, the floor was hard-packed, dried mud. As I entered I moved to one side, crouching while my eyes adjusted to the darkness. What little light there was came from the doorway and a number of small windows higher up the wall. Any floors and stairs that had divided the building were long gone. I could make out half a dozen of the plastic-covered pallets and one of the bright yellow forklift trucks. Now, still crouching low I edged towards it. A shot rang out. 'Come out and show yourself or I'll kill the bitch in front of your eyes, McKinnon,' Mendesa shouted. His voice was close but I couldn't see where he was hiding. A moment of silence then: 'Come out and I'll let her go. If you're the hero you think you are, surely you will risk your life for her.'

I raced for the forklift. A volley of shots rang out but I had reached the cover that the machine provided. It was loaded with a pallet of gold, its forks raised ready to stow it. I climbed up onto it and, my eyes better adjusted to the dark now, took in a view of the whole interior. The space was around sixty by sixty feet. On the far side I could see a line of eight pallets double-stacked. I could see now it was from over there that Mendesa had fired.

As I surveyed the scene someone called out, not Mendesa but a voice I recognised immediately: 'Welcome, McKinnon. This is not personal but you have greatly upset our plans.' Horvat! What the hell was he doing here? But it figured: whether Mendesa was Horvat's stooge or the other way round didn't matter. They were collaborators. And the Russians weren't letting go. Then Mendesa spoke: 'And I have the woman. So your position is not so good right now, is it.'

'Leave him to me,' Horvat said, speaking to Mendesa. 'I have my orders and he is mine. Your job is finished.' No reply came from Mendesa.

My options were limited. I could have tried to negotiate but I wasn't good at bargaining in this kind of situation, as I'd proved outside five minutes earlier. That left me with the Sig, a nine-millimetre pistol with a fifteen-round magazine. And the forklift.

In the dim light I saw a figure pass behind the gap that separated each pair of stacked pallets on the far wall. And I could see there was a narrow corridor formed behind, separating the pallets from the wall. Was it Horvat or Mendesa I saw? Then I heard the chatter of an automatic. A body pitched forward at the end of the row of pallets and lay convulsing before it fell still. They were both big, heavy men but the one lying on his stomach wasn't wearing a *haik* or a turban. He was wearing military fatigues. Why had a pro like Horvat let that happen? Because he trusted Mendesa as an ally in their unholy alliance? But Mendesa was an impulsive maniac who would shoot first and not even bother to ask questions after. No, I thought, more likely Horvat had planned to kill Mendesa on instructions from the GRU and Mendesa had sensed it and fired first. Horvat was not subtle. You could read him like a book. There'd be a reason for how and why it happened, but I'd leave that for another time. If I got out of this alive.

After a while Mendesa spoke: 'There, McKinnon. I've done your job for you. Horvat is dead. The woman is alive, for now, so it's just you and me. I know you want me all to yourself. So come and get me.'

I waited, hesitating without a clear plan of what to do next. Then I heard a shriek and Mariana appeared, hands still bound behind her back, running out of the gap between the pallets and darting over to her left. What she'd done to briefly incapacitate Mendesa I could only guess at. Kneed him in the groin? But as she dashed across the floor seeking cover on my side of the blockhouse, he came out, pausing to spot her. I fired off a few rounds in his direction to distract him then jumped down into the cabin of the big Hyster. I'd used forklifts for cargo work when I was still at sea, though nothing like this heavy-duty beast which could lift twenty tons at a time. I started the engine and lowered the forks so the pallet it was carrying blocked my view but at the same time offered some protection. Swinging it round I aimed at the row of pallets on the far wall where Mendesa was still standing. Above the roar of the engine I heard the chatter of Mendesa's gun as he saw me coming. I heard the sound of rounds punching through the plastic and into the gold bars that were shielding me.

They tell you not to operate a forklift above 10mph but I knew the Hyster would do thirty if you let it. I bounced it across the uneven floor with my foot hard down and jumped from the cab as it hit the bank of pallets on the far side at the point where the gunfire was coming from. I ran through a gap between the stacked bullion and into the corridor behind. The Hyster with its load had crashed into one of the stacks, which was now leaning precariously against the wall. As I peered down the corridor I saw Mendesa coming towards me. I fired again then withdrew ready to get back to the Hyster and ram it into the pallets again. Then I froze and watched as the pallet slipped then toppled into the corridor, crashing to the ground.

My gun was raised but I needn't have bothered. Mendesa's timing had been out. He'd hesitated for a moment too long, wavering over who to go after, me or Mariana. He'd chosen to move forward towards me: bad decision. He'd been crushed underneath the pallet, which had dumped close to two tons of gold bars over him. He was on his back, only his head visible, the rest of him buried under the gold as the plastic wrapping had burst open. Blood was oozing from his eyes, his ears, his mouth and his nose. He was still alive, gasping like a goldfish out of its bowl. I picked up one of the heavy bars. There was no Nazi swastika stamped on it. This gold had been melted down into new bars in Porto after the war, just as Pedro had guessed. I threw it back on the pile.

I was suddenly aware of Mariana standing beside me. A gurgling sound came from Mendesa's throat as his lungs began to fill with blood. We looked down at him as he lay dying, but only for a moment. 'Hoist with your own petard,' I said. The gold he'd thought would bring him the power he craved was slowly killing him. We left him there.

CHAPTER 30

We were at the blockhouse doorway. I'd found a pair of cut-ters from the forklift's toolkit to release Mariana's bonds. She stood beside me, stony-faced in shock. 'Wait here,' I said and stepped outside. A group of Marines were standing beside the entrance to the fort twenty yards away. Conway broke away from them and came over. 'Well?'

'It's done,' I said. 'Horvat too. And you?'

'Done. We've just swept the area. No one left. No survivors.'

'And your men?'

'Five dead,' he said tersely.

I looked back to see Mariana walking slowly towards us. 'Where is he?'

Conway told her bluntly that they'd put Grant in a body bag in the back of one of the Jackals which had been driven into the fort. The bodies of his five men had been placed beside Grant's.

'I would like to see him.'

Conway looked at me and I nodded. The three of us walked over to the vehicle and Conway unzipped the bag to expose the upper half of Grant's body. Mariana looked down at his face. Then she bent down to kiss him and made the sign of the cross on his forehead. She stepped back and walked out of the fort past the trucks and past the Jackals. Then she stopped and stared out at the desert. Her hair blew in the warm breeze which was all that remained of the sandstorm. Behind her the sun was rising, casting sharp shadows from the fort's walls and the blockhouse. After a while I went and stood beside her. 'I'm sorry,' I said uselessly. I wasn't going to tell her yet that that was the way Grant would have wanted to go, in the midst of a covert operation, in the field and not keeling over after overdoing it in the office gym. And I wasn't going to ask her what they'd been doing here. Not yet.

***

'I don't want to hang around here,' said Conway walking over to join us. 'We'll have the local military breathing down our necks if we don't shift this lot out fast. I've ordered the two Hercs in. They're giving an ETA of 0810. That gives us an hour and a half to get the lot packed onto the pallets with the forklifts ready to roll.'

The two C130 Hercules came in, executing what Conway described as a TALO or Tactical Air Landing Operation, the second aircraft a mere two hundred feet above and behind the first. The storm had blown the sand into mounds on what was the airstrip. As the two planes landed the sand was blown into a squall, obliterating everything around them.

'Perfect!' yelled Conway. The planes turned and taxied towards us, stopping thirty or so yards from where we were standing. The pallets that had already been offloaded into the blockhouse were now stacked neatly beside the runway along with those that hadn't already been offloaded from the Zetros trucks. The gold that had collapsed onto Mendesa had been retrieved too. His body was buried in a shallow grave outside the blockhouse along with the Polisarios who had fallen in the battle.

The Zetros trucks would be left behind with one of Conway's units and one of the Jackals. They would set off in convoy to drive back to the coast and rejoin *Buttress*, which was on her way back to rendezvous with them off Nouadhibou. If they encountered the local military at least they wouldn't be caught carrying the gold. But the Reaper would be keeping watch and alert them to any approaching trouble. Their orders were to avoid a confrontation and they were confident they could outrun the Mauritanian army if they had to.

The first plane took off carrying all of the gold. The

second followed with the three Jackals and, seated facing one another behind the cockpit, Conway and his men, Mariana and myself. Grant and Conway's casualties were laid on the floor in body bags – a reminder that the op would never be judged a success. Certainly, Conway and his men didn't look like they thought it was. The atmosphere was subdued and I fell to thinking about Grant. Most of his career had been spent behind a desk, not in the field. He knew he'd slipped up by telling Cordeiro of the CIA's plans and felt the need to set things right. But if he hadn't fallen so heavily for Mariana would he have put them both in harm's way like that, and then met with such a violent death? I looked across at her, wondering if she was thinking the same thing.

***

Montijo Air Base is a military facility conveniently located on the opposite bank of the Rio Tejo from Lisbon. One day it will serve as Lisbon's second civilian airport but for now it was home to three Portuguese Navy transport squadrons and a helicopter search and rescue base.

After a thirteen hundred mile flight north we landed there late afternoon. Since we were carrying one and a half billion dollars' worth of gold for delivery to the Banco de Portugal, security was tight, not least because although the gold had lain undisturbed in the Banco Imperio's Porto vaults for the last seventy-three years, the question of who it actually belonged to was the subject of much heated debate.

Eventually, after two tallies and in the presence of several Portuguese, British and US officials and various military personnel, I signed the lot over and it was transferred to a fleet of armoured security vans. The convoy departed for Lisbon escorted by half a dozen VBL army vehicles.

'Why didn't they just load the lot onto a barge and tow it across?' I asked Conway.

He allowed himself a grim smile. 'You would think of a maritime solution wouldn't you.'

We watched the two Hercules take off, heading east back to Akrotiri. I turned to Mariana: 'What now?'

'He was a good man,' she said. 'I thought we had a future together.' Then she slipped her hand into the pocket of her jacket and pulled out a pendant. It was set in gold and hung from a gold chain. Smiling faintly she swung it gently to and fro. 'He got this back for me.'

'What is it?'

'A black star sapphire,' she said handing it to me. It was heavy, a huge oval-shaped stone. I held it up so the light from the setting sun caught it and the six-rayed star appeared, shifting mystically at its centre.

'Is this yours?'

'It is what Mendesa took when he murdered my father. My mother had left it with him when we fled from Kazunda, as a reminder of their love, but as a symbol of the new nation's hopes too. It is called the Black Reef Star because that is where it was found – in the basalt rock on Black Reef, below the fort. The sea had eroded the rock around it and left it exposed. It is seven hundred and forty carat, probably the largest black star sapphire in the world.'

She sighed. 'My grandfather was the last governor of Kazunda before independence. Did you not know that? He passed it down. I knew Mendesa had it. Grant retrieved it for me. Now I shall take it back to Kazunda and entrust it to Nzinga. It is the nation's crown jewel.'

I handed it back to her. 'What happened, Mariana? What were you doing there? I thought Grant was over in the States.'

'He came back straight from America and met me here in Lisbon. He knew where Mendesa was taking the gold. And he knew how important it was for me to see that man's life finished.'

'How did he know?'

'He had his contacts. He said he was still in charge of the case. He wanted to help me.'

'And this?' I said, touching the stone in her hand.

'Mendesa wanted me. He knew that I knew he had the stone. He knew where to find me and he lured us into the desert with the promise of the stone.'

'Grant was in charge of the case,' I said. 'And in his

shoes I would have wanted to be there at the end too.'

We talked there until it fell dark and Pedro rolled up in his old Seat. He took us over the 25 de Abril Bridge back into the city, dropping me off at the Hospital da Luz. We drew up and Mariana got out of the car. She reached up and kissed me. 'Now go to your *amante*,' she said, smiling. 'But do not forget me either, Angus. And be careful out there in your strange world. I do not want to lose another good friend.'

EPILOGUE

Despite the sunshine, it was a bitterly cold day in New England. There had been some doubt as to where Grant Douglas was to be buried. As a serving CIA officer there would have been a place for him at Arlington National Cemetery, but when his will and testimony were finally read his wishes were clear. He wanted to be buried beside his wife. Later there would be a star carved onto the CIA Memorial Wall in Langley, honouring Grant as a CIA officer who had died in the line of service. His name would be listed, but place and cause of death would be recorded as unknown, for security reasons. So we'd come to attend his funeral in Greenwich, Connecticut: Amber Dove, Claire, Ben Wood, Phyllis and three other CMM staff members, a small crowd of old friends and relatives, and half a dozen colleagues from Langley. Mariana wasn't there. Pedro sent me a message saying she was moving on with her life. I didn't blame her.

We were leaving when one of the CIA guys came over and took my arm. He was older than the others, closer to

Grant's age. 'Can I have a word?' he asked. We stood under some fine old oak trees which guarded the edges of the cemetery. The other mourners were moving away towards their cars: black figures contrasting with the bright sunshine in this immaculately maintained sanctuary.

'He was a great guy,' he said. 'I knew him in 'Nam. We stayed in touch – through work but as buddies too. He thought a lot of you by the way.'

'And I of him,' I replied, realising how much I was already missing Grant and feeling a twinge of regret over the acerbic attitude I'd often shown towards him.

'Oh,' the spook added, 'and just for the record, that hit on Cordeiro: it wasn't us.'

'Who then? Moscow?'

He just shrugged. 'You guys have a safe trip home now.'

***

Captain Luca Babic's body had finally been released from the mortuary in Lisbon. Sonia Babic had arranged for her husband to be buried in a cemetery near their home in Thessaloniki and, following some sensitive negotiations with the local Greek Orthodox priest, it was agreed he would receive a joint Catholic and Orthodox funeral. I'd talked this through with Pedro who had arranged for Father Manuel from the Apostleship of the Sea in Setubal to come over, expenses paid, to perform a Catholic rite of committal; a gesture that both surprised and touched Sonia Babic.

Benny Carasso was there, and Zoe and I had come up from Piraeus. 'Was I right?' Benny asked on our way to the *makaria*, the traditional post-funeral meal or wake to celebrate Babic's life.

'About what?'

'What did I say? You got the Portuguese, you got the Chinese, you got the Russkies and you got the Yanks. Who was it?'

'Actually, in one way or another, they were all involved, Benny.' And as we sat down for our meal I told him what I could about the case and how it had unfolded.

***

For a fortnight each year, so the myth goes, Alcyone the kingfisher made her nest on the beach and laid her eggs. During this time her father Aeolus, god of the winds, calmed the wind and waves so she could lay the eggs in safety. For Greeks it has come to mean any time of peace – a bright interval amidst adversity. But it's always a pleasant surprise when the weather takes a turn for the better in the middle of winter, even if only for a week or two. Apparently, the meteorological reason for this phenomenon is that barometric pressures between southern and northern Europe equalise on or around the shortest day of the year. Fortunately, the arrival of the halcyon days coincided with Claire's arrival on the island and for a fortnight we enjoyed mild, sunny weather.

She was eager to see how work on the olive mill was progressing but it was an informal debriefing session too. We sat out on one of the *plaka* terraces that had been built on the southern side of the house. The olive trees had been stripped of their fruit in November and had produced my first harvest of oil. Now their silvery green foliage and the hills that flanked the grove framed the view of the sea, which glittered below us in the late morning sunlight.

Claire had made a good recovery and was now able to walk without the cast or the crutches, though she kept a walking pole handy too. We talked through the events of the last few weeks. She would often ask me to repeat one aspect or another in more detail. She recorded these sessions and took notes. When we got to Mariana and Grant, she said: 'I still can't quite believe they were an item. I mean, it was all rather sudden wasn't it?'

'Wasn't it for us too?' I replied casting my mind back to when I'd first met Claire. 'You meet someone in dangerous circumstances and a bond can be forged very quickly. They recognised something in each other: a mutual resolve. More than that though: they were both looking for someone even though they may not have known it.'

'Yes, of course.'

At another point she asked me to describe Nzinga. 'I'd love to meet her, she sounds fascinating. And Mariana too.'

'You probably will,' I said, standing up. The IMTF didn't like to lose touch with people of influence whom they'd helped out of difficult situations. 'You should go down to Kazunda with Mariana sometime. She told me Nzinga had already renegotiated the contract with Sea-En and was in Beijing talking to the Chinese about a new railway network for the country.'

'I might just do that. By the way, do you think Mariana would make a good asset for us?'

'I'm not sure,' I said. 'She saw what people like us have to do to reach the desired outcome. We say the end justifies the means but it's not always very honourable is it. She might want nothing more to do with us. Can I get you anything? More coffee?'

'I'd love a glass of wine.'

I walked into the house to get a bottle from the fridge, the contrast between the dazzling sunshine and the gloom of the interior momentarily blinding me. My mind went back to Mariana and what a strong, resourceful woman she was. I uncorked the bottle, placed it in a cooler and, grabbing a couple of glasses, returned to the terrace.

'You know, now I come to think about it,' I said, 'perhaps she'd make a damn good agent. She's smart, pragmatic, gutsy.'

Claire had stood up and was staring out to sea. 'Umm. If I went down there with Mariana to meet Nzinga I could assess her at the same time.'

'Why not?'

She turned and took the glasses from me, placing them on the old wooden table. 'You are an angel looking after me like this. I can't think of anywhere better to convalesce than here.'

'You didn't always feel this way about the island,' I said as I poured the wine.

'I know I didn't, but a girl can change her mind can't she? *Yamas!*

'*Yamas!*

She reached up and kissed me. I held her gently. 'Hold me tight, darling. I told you, I'm strong now.'

ABOUT THE AUTHOR

Nick Elliott began his career as a boarding agent attending ships in Edinburgh's port of Leith. He moved to Hong Kong in the Seventies and lived throughout the Far East for twenty years before relocating to Greece and eventually back to the UK.

Throughout, he has worked, lived and breathed shipping and more than a few of the events described in his books are inspired by his own experiences. He is a Fellow of the Institute of Chartered Shipbrokers.

Married with two daughters, he divides his time between Scotland and a Greek island.

Sea of Gold was his first novel. It was followed by Dark Ocean, Black Reef and in 2021, The Code, a prequel to the first three.

ACKNOWLEDGEMENTS

My thanks to Helen Bleck, my editor, and to Doctor Jane Stanford, Rear Admiral (ret'd) Roger Lockwood, Flight Lieutenant Paul Bevan and Steve Cameron for their input on matters medical, naval, airborne and Africa, respectively. Also to author friends, Craig Russell and Peter A. Flannery for their advice and support.

IF YOU ENJOYED THIS BOOK

If you enjoyed reading *Black Reef* I'd be very grateful if you would leave a short review on Amazon. Good reviews help other readers find and enjoy a book.

If you would like to get in touch, please contact me via my website: **www.nickelliott.org**

And thanks for buying the book.

Nick Elliott

SEA OF GOLD, DARK OCEAN,
BLACK REEF AND THE CODE

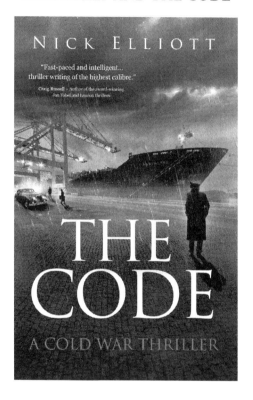

Buy The Code here: https://amzn.to/3lGVtDq

What readers have said about The Code

"The Angus McKinnon thrillers are set within the maritime industry. Speaking as an ex seafarer, Nick Elliott's many years of industry experience shine through, bringing credibility to the scenes he sets and depth to the profiles of the main characters. A gripping read, I have enjoyed all of the Angus McKinnon series."

***

"Another cracking read from Nick Elliott. Once again, the story, a prequel, moves with breathless pace and, in common with his other books in this series, he guides us across an enormously wide geographic landscape - this time from Lebanon, Latvia, through the Balkans and ending up in the West Indies. It's also good to know now how Angus McKinnon became the maritime sleuth we know so well from the first three books. Very highly recommended."

***

"Just finished Nick Elliott's 4th book, The Code. A great prequel to his Angus McKinnon trilogy. His writing gets better and better."

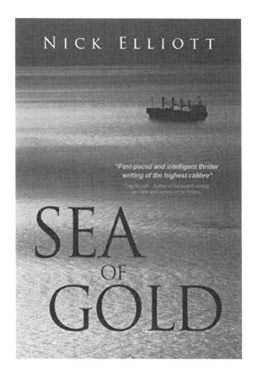

Buy Sea of Gold here: http://amzn.to/1jkQUYT

What readers have said about Sea of Gold

"Nick Elliott ticks all the boxes in this fast-paced yarn, with a keen eye for descriptive detail and solidly drawn characters. The first-person narrative, complete with ironic internal asides, is the perfect vehicle for a thoughtful and witty style that draws us swiftly into the shoes of its protagonist, a credible and consistent character."

***

"A unique twist on the spy detective thriller featuring impeccably researched action that is set in a host of well invoked locations. I look forward with intrigue to Angus McKinnon's further adventures."

***

"This is a first rate, well-constructed first novel which benefits from the author's learned insight into the maritime business world and his familiarity with interesting parts of the world. In addition he introduces us to some interesting characters who fortunately survive the tricky circumstances in which they find themselves and who we look forward to meeting again in the sequel(s). I predict a successful future for Nick Elliott who will I feel sure continue to set his stories in fascinating parts of the world. I thoroughly enjoyed this book."

***

"In the tradition of Eric Ambler, this is a well written crime novel. What starts out as a case of insurance fraud turns into a battle of international intrigue."

***

"A fascinating and very well-written story in a world I knew nothing about, commercial shipping. If you are a mystery fan, enjoy reading about international intrigue, appreciate well-developed complex characters and are curious about or fascinated by the high seas, this is for you. A powerful first book."

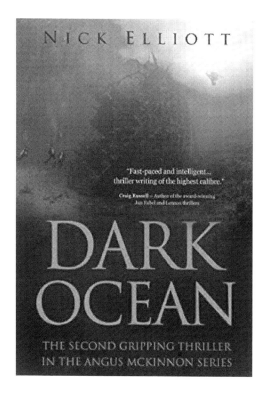

Buy Dark Ocean here: http://amzn.to/2vIPRyJ

What readers have said about Dark Ocean

"This really is an expertly researched, very well-written and fast-paced international thriller. The protagonist, Angus McKinnon, is a character with real dimension and credibility, which is something often lacking in this kind of fiction. You believe in him, and you believe in the streets, alleys and seaways he travels: every location is atmospherically and authentically created as your drawn deeper and deeper into a dark world where nothing is what is seems. Superb book."

"Felt like I was back in the Orient when I was reading this book. I could easily visualize every aspect of the author's descriptions of people and places. So many plot twists. Thoroughly enjoyed this book."

***

"Dark Ocean hit landmarks with which I am familiar (Kowloon and Hong Kong), and I loved all the interesting tidbits of shipping detail, description of ports, and customs of the locals, including the exchange of commerce with Japan. This book grabs your attention immediately then quickly widens to that of international intrigue that includes the collusion of a major cabal in what might be a hostile takeover--a far-reaching takeover. The threatening organization is deeply rooted and far ranging and has Angus flying to retrieve information from sources he thought well buried in his past--only to have to retrieve, relive, and sort. But as with any good thriller, a piece of the puzzle only leads to hints of acquiring the next piece."

***

"The book is a well-plotted, multi-layered suspense with slightly rogue alpha male management style being ever more deeply entangled in MI6 as they coordinate between agencies. There is so much (fictional?) information here reading as gospel that it becomes scary."

***

"Nick Elliott has done it again. Following Sea of Gold he has come up with an equally gripping, intelligent and well-paced thriller in Dark Ocean. Set in the shipping industry which he knows intimately and in countries which he knows like a native and in which you can feel the pulse of the street life, the plot leads you on in an unputdownable way. Once started you have to read on to the end. The characters, especially the female ones, are excellently crafted and true to life. Who knew that shipping could be so interesting?"

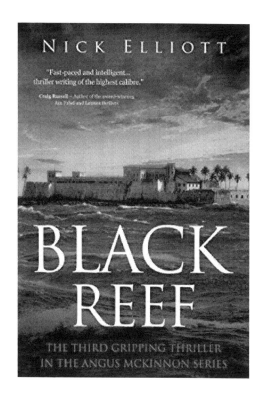

Buy Black Reef here: https://amzn.to/2zVBo4e

What readers have said about Black Reef

"I have now completed the Angus McKinnon trilogy and they get better and better. Like the previous two, Black Reef covers a tremendously wide geographical canvas written with Nick Elliott's intimate knowledge of those parts of the world together with the people who live there. So the book is fascinating on that count alone; add the breadth of the story, the excitement and suspense at almost every page and the quality of the writing and you have an action thriller amongst the very best.

This book stands alone from the previous two, but if you haven't read them yet - do!"

***

"Nick Elliott does it again, his work just gets better and better. If you have read Nick's first two books this is a must read. If you haven't read the others then you have three must read books to enjoy. Can't wait for the next one."

***

"I really enjoyed meeting Angus again and being drawn into this third thrilling case. What a great trilogy. I particularly enjoy the depth of knowledge Nick Elliott shows when it comes to the different locations Angus finds himself in, as well as the fascinating mysteries of the shipping world. What great reads!"

Or buy the trilogy box set here: https://amzn.to/2Ov8WhE

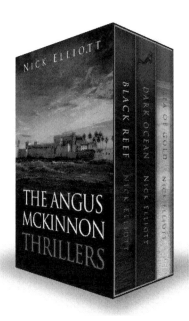

Printed in Great Britain
by Amazon

14885245R00178